OPEN SEASON

Once you're used to a city, the early-morning quiet of a small town is beyond belief. The only noises I heard were a truck backfiring on a side street and a stone I must have kicked skittering near my feet. I was headed toward the Crystal Café in the middle of the block, glancing casually at the merchandise dimly visible in security-lit stores.

This time when the truck backfired I realized I hadn't heard any motor noise. This time when the stone skittered, I saw it chip out of the brick next to me.

I flattened into the doorway of the five-and-dime shop, hand inside my coat. I couldn't bring myself to draw my gun; it seemed too unreal. No one else had run outside; no one had called out or noticed. A block and a half away a woman with a stroller pushed across Main Street, jaywalking. Here that usually wasn't dangerous. I opened my mouth to shout to her, then shut it as a web of cracks appeared in the glass door behind and above me. . . .

Also by Nick O'Donohoe
APRIL SNOW
WIND CHILL

OPEN SEASON
A NATHAN PHILLIPS MYSTERY

Nick O'Donohoe

PaperJacks LTD.

TORONTO   NEW YORK

AN ORIGINAL

PaperJacks

OPEN SEASON

PaperJacks LTD.

330 STEELCASE RD. E., MARKHAM, ONT. L3R 2M1
210 FIFTH AVE., NEW YORK, N.Y. 10010

PaperJacks edition published August 1986

Cover design: Vincent Priore

This is a work of fiction in its entirety. Any resemblance to actual people, places or events is purely coincidental.

ISBN 0-7701-0476-2
Printed in Canada

To Kit, Judy, Jenny, and Emily

ACKNOWLEDGMENTS

Some of the bee culture information used in this book is from *The ABC and XYZ of Bee Culture* (Medina, Ohio: 1975 edition), by A.I. Root, revised and reissued by generations of the Root family.

Chapter One

We bumped into each other in the library, which shows you don't have to meet at theaters, concerts, or singles bars. Ironically, I was working on a divorce case.

I was sitting behind a stack of phone directories and newspaper articles about the Ukraine League, looking for the friends of Terry Selinoff. She was sitting behind a stack of *Newsweek* magazines, Sunday supplements, and back issues of *The Wall Street Journal*; I wasn't sure what she was looking for. She jumped when I said hello, so I added, "Sorry, I didn't mean to startle you."

"That's all right. Probably too much coffee." She looked confused, almost unsure. That wasn't like her . . .

"I've wanted to talk to you for some time." I stopped, struggling. "Last time we met, I wasn't too friendly. I was kind of jumpy then —"

"You had reasons to be, if I can believe the papers. You're Nathan Phillips, aren't you?" I nodded, and she held out a hand. "I'm Anne Commenger." The reasons were better than she knew. The IRA, the FBI, and assorted blackmailers, killers, and corpses aren't exactly calming. It wouldn't be tactful to say so, but I'd thought this woman might — like everyone else back then — want to kill me.

"Thanks for understanding, but good reasons don't excuse bad manners."

"Don't worry about it. Is it always that exciting, being a private detective?"

"Sometimes. I like the dull parts, myself. How is running an ad agency?"

"You remembered." She smiled, and I was glad I had. "It isn't bad. It's crazy, but it's mine."

"That's how I feel. It's nice being self-employed." It was something I could never have explained to most of my friends. "You seem pretty calm right now."

Actually, she didn't, and I wondered why.

"This is the peaceful part. No clients, no interviews, no market surveys —"

"What kinds of markets?"

She opened her mouth, shut it, and looked at me. "Sure you want to start me? I might take a while."

"Say 'go.' "

My, what a smile. I meet ten or twenty people a day, and none of them smile like that. "I just might."

"Could we talk over dinner?" She was hesitating. "At six o'clock?" I added coaxingly, "I promise I'll ask about markets."

She checked her watch. "Could we make it earlier? It's four-thirty now."

"Quarter to five for drinks, dinner at five-thirty?"

She glanced at her watch. "Much better. How about five? I have to keep to a schedule."

"Sure. Let me make a phone call. I'll be right back."

"Calling the police?" She looked half serious.

"Don't need to." I looked all serious, which I wasn't. "I'm tracking a missing man."

I went to the pay phone downstairs, hoping to impress

her by finding him on the first try. I called my first address, squinting at the name, and said, "Van? Vannie? This is Nathan." I tried to sound like a veteran of a long-gone purge. "You don't know me, but Terry used to talk about you. Sure, Terry Selinoff. Yep, used to say what a hell of a guy you were. Sure, those were his very words. What? Oh."

Back upstairs Annie said, "Find him?"

"No, but I learned more about him." I told her how I'd started the call.

"What did you find out?"

"Terry Selinoff doesn't speak English. I don't think it's that funny."

After a moment she said, "I'm sorry."

"It's okay to laugh. I would if it hadn't happened to me." I wished that I'd impressed her more. "Can we go now? I need a drink."

She ordered a margarita. "There's barely any summer left."

"Sounds sensible. Make it two." The waitress left. "We should have talked at the beginning of the summer. Bernie — a friend of mine; he loves parties — sponsored National Margarita Day."

"What nation, and what day?"

"His own nation, the weekend on or after June twelfth. He says there ought to be a holiday between Memorial Day and the Fourth of July, just so we all know it's summer."

"Good idea. I couldn't take a whole day of margaritas, though."

"You have to take it slowly, if at all. One year we made two bad mistakes: Bernie mixed, and we were thirsty. We knew we were in trouble when Bernie put a sombrero on Dave — another friend — and told him to be colorful. Dave did a hat dance and sang a Bohemian drinking song."

"Your friends sound fun."

"They are that. I'd like you to meet Bernie. Don't panic if he proposes."

"Is he likely to?" So I explained about Bernie's hobby of getting engaged, and she told a story about one of her college friends (it was funny even if you didn't know the people), and it was time for dinner.

Annie shivered, even though we were inside looking out. "I'm glad I took my jacket this morning. It's cold tonight."

"The woolly bears say we'll have a long winter. This feels like mid-October."

"It's not far off. We should go to a college football game."

"Nah. We're too old for that."

"Maybe. I still like football, though."

"This weekend?"

"Sure."

I liked that. It takes a lot of pressure off a first date if you know there might be a second.

We had coffee and brandy after dinner — something I mostly don't do, I hate feeling jittery and drunk at once.

Annie — Anne — sipped frequently, almost mechanically. Apparently I made her nervous. Was it because I'd been so spooked when we met last winter? "You work alone?"

"What? Oh, no. Actually, it's a partnership, and we employ four people. But Laurie — my partner — lets me have my head, set my hours, and work alone. We like it that way."

"I know what you mean; so do I. Once I had a partner. As a matter of fact, he founded the firm."

She nodded, looking at me intently. I stopped. "Is something wrong?"

"Not at all. Go ahead. How did you meet him?"

"He was a friend of my dad's. I knocked around without doing much after college — odd jobs, some sales, a little work for an insurance company — and Dad dragged me in and introduced me. Roy was looking for a partner, and I had okay skills, even if I wasn't terribly motivated."

"Roy?"

"Roy Cartley. We turned into good friends, and — you sure something isn't wrong?"

"Nothing. Go on."

"Anyway, Roy taught me most of what I know about investigating — everything but how to work alone. I learned that after he died."

"How did he die?" When she asked that, I knew something was wrong. She sounded as though she was testing, not inquiring. The evening was going sour, and I wasn't sure why. Suddenly I realized how important this date was for me.

"Car accident. A drunk driver hit him. Listen, we don't need to talk about it."

"We do." She clenched and unclenched her napkin, not looking at it or at me. "I've been waiting for months to see you again. I was afraid to go to your office. Last spring, in a restaurant, I overheard two men. They were talking about your partner's death. Nate, he was murdered."

Chapter Two

After a few seconds she opened her eyes and said, "Show your hands."

"Fists." But I showed them. "You can't do this. I got used to Roy's death." It sounded silly, but I added, "I was having a good time tonight."

"What was I supposed to do, keep it to myself?"

"You've got to be wrong. I saw the accident report. I saw the schlemiel that did it plea-bargain and get a minimal sentence."

"That was planned. The whole thing was planned, but I think the sentence was shorter than even they expected. They sounded upset." She added, looking at my face, "I'm sorry. Maybe I should have waited longer, or maybe I should have called you right after I finished hunting through back issues of the newspapers for your name." I should have known; she'd mentioned reading about me.

"I don't believe it. No; I believe you, but I don't believe *them*." I was shaking. "Did they say why?"

"Of course not. They already knew why."

"Sure." The waitress, with admirable delicacy, set the check exactly between us and glided off before the fight. "I'll get the check."

"Let me."

"We can split it."

"That's just foolish." She was pretty upset herself. "Look, I feel rotten. At least let me buy dinner."

"Tell you what. Can we go out again? You pay then."

"What?"

"It's a ploy. Then we'll go out again."

"We already said we're going to a football game."

"After the game, then."

She almost smiled. "Nate, how can you do this now?"

"First things first." I shook my head. "I think it's first things first. Well." I pulled the check toward myself and flinched quietly as she paid the tip. Some things take getting used to.

"Where are we going?"

"See a friend." I drove automatically, the way people head home when there's almost been a disaster.

"You sure about this?"

"Positive. Don't you want to know what I'm doing?" I rang the doorbell.

"Why?"

He came to the door after three rings and a knock. In a bathrobe Jon doesn't look like a homicide cop. On the other hand, his bathrobe was dark blue; maybe, now that he wore a coat and tie to work, he needed blues at home.

He looked me up and down. "You're sober. Why'd you stay till I answered?" He saw Anne and added more quietly, "Sorry to yell."

I said, "Why the bathrobe?"

"I look silly naked."

"No doubt — I would have called first —"

"You got that right. You should have." He started closing the door.

I stuck my foot in it. "Anne, this is Jon Pederson; Jon,

this is Anne Commenger. Anne overheard two men talking about how Roy Cartley was murdered.''

Quiet. My God, the nights were still in this neighborhood. No cars, no stereos; just widows and widowers and older couples who wanted nothing but peace.

He stepped back, we stepped in, and the door slammed shut. "When?"

"March, this year. In a restaurant, at about six p.m." She sounded calm, but I knew she wasn't.

"March, huh? It's September. Where've you been?"

"I was afraid. Besides, the papers said it was an accident. How could I spring this on someone?"

"You can spring it on the police."

"If you want." I wished she hadn't said that. It would only make Jon mad, and he was being rough already.

"And you didn't want. Terrific. Who were these guys?"

"I'm not sure."

"What'd they look like?"

"Short, late forties to early fifties, thinning gray hair —"

"We'll put out an APB on Rotary International. Where?"

"Carmine's."

"Your date hear them?"

"I was alone."

He stepped forward, but she didn't back up. "They were kidding you."

"I was in the next booth. They didn't know."

"You misheard." He stepped still closer.

"I couldn't have. They were talking too loudly. They were drunk." She tensed, but stood her ground. Jon didn't back up, either. Neither of them seemed to know I was there.

He shouted, almost in her face, "And you? How drunk were you, out alone at Happy Hour?"

"Shut up!" To my surprise, maybe to Anne's, he did. She went on, her voice shaky, "I came to you. Late, but I came. A friend of Nate's was murdered. Start with that.''

Jon stared at her. He moved his mouth. He waved his arms, but none of his gestures made sense.

Then, all at once and without warning, he started to cry.

Willa came out in a fuzzy red K-Mart bathrobe; as always, she looked great. "I heard shouts. Jon, what — ?" He buried his face in his hands and dropped to the couch. She was by him without seeming to have walked over, hands on his shoulders. She looked up at Anne and me. "Shame on you." No questions.

I said, "Willa, it's rough news. Turns out —"

Jon said into his hands, "It's my fault. All the way. I never checked, I never asked, I told someone else to do it —"

What could I say? "It's not your fault, Jon. Roy wouldn't have expected —"

"*I* would." He thumped the couch arm. "Don't you see that? It's me. He was my friend."

"Who are you talking about?" Willa stroked his shoulders, but looked at us. "Roy's been dead for —" And it hit her. "Oh, no. You can't mean — Oh, no." Her hand clenced on Jon's arm; he reached up and grabbed her fingers. Ten white knuckles worked against each other.

Anne said flatly, "They're friends of your partner's."

"I should have told you. It didn't seem important." That sounded stupid even to me. "Jon had to know."

"Why?" Willa wasn't crying. She'd cry later, behind a closed door. I'd overheard her once, when Jon was wounded at an arrest; she didn't know I knew. "We really had to know?"

I sat down. "I knew."

Anne said tightly, "I should have forgotten the whole thing."

"That's no good." Willa let go of Jon's hand. "Some things you can't forget. Jonny never can. What's your part in all this?" Anne told her. Willa nodded. "You couldn't help it. It was Roy's murder, but your accident."

Jon said muffledly, "We don't know he was murdered."

We all looked at him. He brought his head up. "But we'll find out." He pulled a Kleenex out of his bathrobe pocket. "Everything."

Anne walked over and squatted down by the couch. "I'm truly sorry, Mr. Pederson. I had no idea you were anything but a policeman in all this."

"Believe me, honey," Willa said proudly, "he's a cop." I always thought policemen's wives were supposed to hate their husbands' work. "But he was Roy's friend. He'll find out."

"That's what friends are for." Even as I said it, I felt foolish.

"No." Jon was angry again. It's not personal. It's — it's like somebody shot a cop."

"No, it isn't. But we'll find out."

Jon growled, almost normally, "Can't we even agree when we agree?" I felt better immediately.

Willa said, unexpectedly, "I haven't been introduced," so I introduced Anne and Willa. "Pleased to meet you, Anne. I wish it had been at a better time."

"Me, too. This wan't my idea. We were just finishing dinner —"

"You're not one of Nate's clients, then." Willa gave me a look more probing than Jon's Third Degree Face.

Suddenly I couldn't talk fast enough. "We met at the library and decided to have drinks and an early dinner."

"And now it's nearly ten. And a week night."

"Nearly ten?" I looked at my watch. "You're right."

Willa gave me the Third Degree Smile. "Some dinner."

I tried to dodge. "That's not so late. Since when does Jon go to bed at ten?"

He sputtered. Willa smiled quietly and slipped her hand over his. Annie laughed at me, and I stumbled toward the door.

Annie stood in front of Jon. "Mr. Pederson, this never should have happened. I'm sorry. It's my fault."

He almost smiled. "Don't you worry. It's mine, and Nate's."

"Partly, I guess. I'm sorry I didn't speak up sooner, and that it hurt you so when I did. I knew it was murder, though, and I couldn't just let it go." She added, "I knew." I don't think she realized she was echoing me.

Now he did smile. "My kind of gal. Make Nate bring you back when it's not business." He turned away before we were out the door.

The ride back to Anne's was quiet; both of us were exhausted. Finally she said, "He looks like the kind of man who'd apologize for crying. He didn't, though, and I'm glad."

"Jon isn't sorry he cried." I sure was. "Annie, can you see why he had to know? Why I couldn't just let you walk into his office and dictate it to someone who would throw it on his desk?"

"So Willa would be there." Funny how it was always easier to call Willa by her first name than it was Jon.

"Sure. And me." I was surprised at myself. "Somewhere along the line Jon and I became good friends. Certainly, he's been a friend to me. I've always wanted to be one back."

"I'll bet you're a good one."

"Tonight wasn't my best."

"I'd hope not, if we're going out again."

"Are we?" I didn't add, "Still?"

Neither did she. "I asked you first."

"You didn't exactly — ah, what the hell. Yes, I sure hope so, anyway. Promise we don't say a word about Roy or about anything connected with — with him?"

"You're on." She added, "Why did Mr. Pederson take it so hard?"

I thought before answering. "After Roy's death I found

out Jon hadn't even read the accident report. My guess is that Jon was asked to investigate, but pulled some strings and got someone else — I bet I know who, a kid in Homicide who's good but needs experience — to check into the accident. Jon was probably afraid of being too hard on the other driver, afraid of making a drunk driver out to be a cold-blooded assassin.''

"Wow. And now he feels he let a friend down. Friends,'' she corrected, looking at me. "Can you make him feel better?''

I doubted it. "I'll try. Know what? Jon was right; you're nice. And tough.'' I stretched. "This was easily the strangest first date I ever went on. Think we should do this again next week?''

She looked bleakly at me. "Frankly, Nate, I *would* miss it for anything.''

After I'd been home half an hour the phone rang. Marlowe, just in from a yowl and sleepy, barely twitched. "Hello?''

"She say anything else?''

"No. I didn't ask, Jon. She'll give her statement tomorrow.''

"And you'll be hitting your office records.'' He wasn't ordering me, but he wasn't asking, either. I was surprised.

"You think it was business related?''

"Don't you?''

"Jon, Roy and I doubled up on every case then. Whoever killed him would've killed me, if it was business.''

"Maybe they got sloppy, or you got lucky. Both have happened before.''

I didn't like to think how true that was. "I'll look, Jon. All that year's files are inactive; if you want I'll bring them in.''

"Wait till I've seen Anne. If she has something real, and

you don't, bring them in. I may look at them after you, anyway."

"Nobody could look those records over more carefully than I will."

"Watch me. Nate, how well do you know this woman?"

"Not at all."

"But you believe her?"

Did I? I thought for a minute. "I don't know why I do —"

"I mean ignoring that fact that you like her."

"I'm not even sure of that, yet."

"The hell you're not. And you do believe her."

"I do. But I think I like her because I believe her, not the other way around."

"We'll know tomorrow. Had a good time, did you?"

"Right up till the bomb dropped, sure. But I think you had a wilder night by staying at home."

He chuckled. "Talk to you later."

He was gone. I stared at the phone. I was involved in a murder, I was heartsick over one friend and angry for another, and the wonderful time just before it felt like days ago.

Chapter Three

I was deliberate in the office, ritualistically setting up the coffee, sharpening all my pencils and going over my calendar as though it held advice on how to live forever. (Actually, it told me my business Mastercharge needed paying.) After stalling as long as I could, I went to the closet.

I've never used it for my coat; I have a rack in the waiting room for that. Nobody would steal that coat.

The closet was full of dead storage boxes, card files held shut with string and containing all the business that wasn't likely to repeat. All of it was dated by year, some years alphabetized by clients' names, though in a business tied to divorces, frauds and aliases, last names didn't mean that much.

I stared at the box for a minute or two. It was near the top; in the back and below were twenty or thirty old boxes of Roy's, only about a fifth of them from years when I'd been with him. I felt like opening any box but the right one and doing a rainy day's research.

I shifted the box for a while. I cut the string. I played with the frayed ends, thinking what my cat could do with them, then gave up. I couldn't stall until five o'clock. I lifted the lid and read the names off slowly and carefully: "Bostwick, Adrian. Bowman, 'Handy Andy.' " And, further back, "Grey, Elizabeth (deceased). Gordon, Harry." And "Kirk, Lyle."

I was kidding myself again. I reached in and picked out "Cartley, Roy," without having to search. I'd felt cheap filing it with the clients, but I'd have felt sillier keeping it with the current work. Anything two years old had no right on my desk. I also took out that year's journal — about a third of it in Roy's handwriting and the rest in mine — and set that beside the file.

I wanted to start with the journal, but that was stupid. How would I know what to look for? I grabbed some coffee (normally I'd rather have tea), opened the accident report and waded in.

Roy had been driving north on 35W when a drunk driver named Stanley Colfax came off the University Avenue exit ramp and smashed into him in a drunken attempt to merge. Colfax had merged Roy into the guardrail, which bounced him into the path of the next car.

The driver of that car, a dancer named Walter Johnson, had tried to brake, but there was no time. He received a bad whiplash and a concussion. Roy's neck snapped, either then or when he'd been hit the first time. The whole thing took fifteen seconds.

Johnson's career in a local troupe, a struggling group on a now-defunct federal grant, was over. I'd scrawled a later note on the report; Johnson had brought a civil suit against Colfax and, amazingly, had lost. He couldn't prove that Colfax's drunken driving rather than his attempt to save his and Roy's lives had caused the neck injury. I wondered what he was doing now.

Colfax had lived in a not-too-fashionable neighborhood in St. Paul, the kind where furnished apartments come with winos. The ambulance crew found Roy dead, Johnson unconscious and Colfax belching bubbles over the steering wheel. There was a fifth of bourbon, the cap off, draining into Colfax's floor mat.

Quite a bit had drained into Colfax. His test — though there were problems about it being admitted as evidence — showed his alcohol count was way up there, the equivalent of a six-ounce glass of bourbon in the last hour. His reflexes were nothing. His background was about what you'd expect: not a bad man, from a little town south of the Cities, till he'd hit the bottle and the bottle had hit back. He'd come crawling to the Twin Cities on his merry way to being a derelict. Partway through his crawl, he'd hit Roy.

I thought about that. How far through his crawl? I made a note of his old address and his landlord's name. Maybe the building was still there, and the landlord. That part of St. Paul was so run down it might be hard to tell them apart by now.

Fine. That was something, at least. I read another handwritten scrawl on the file: Colfax had plea-bargained, and a hard bargain at that. Some kind of criminal negligence with a three-to-five-year sentence, of which he'd drawn three and served one and a half. He'd had a good lawyer, and this was before MADD and SADD — those groups that think drunk-driving penalties are too lenient. Can't imagine why.

I didn't have Colfax's current address, since I hadn't thought I'd ever need it. I didn't even have his old home address in Belle View, Minnesota — just the name of the town, and a statement that he'd come up to the Twin Cities a few months before.

I shook my head. It was a hell of a thing to lose your best friend, and worse to lose a good man because he got hit by some jerk nearly on April Fool's Day.

I snapped my head up. April Fool's. First of the month. He'd just moved to the city a few months ago . . . I could have asked by phone, but I wanted to get out. With luck I could stay out till lunch. I drove over to the building Colfax used to live in, savoring the sunshine. There wouldn't be many more days like this.

The building was a four-story blockhouse with porches sagging off its front, grimy, formerly white stucco chipping off its walls and a torn shade in every window but the one that had no shade at all. Most of the shades were down even by day. That wasn't a healthy sign.

On a cracked pane of the front door was a sign saying uncompromisingly: "WARNING: These Premises Protected Night and Day by Frederick Security Systems, Inc." I grinned; I knew Fred. The only service he sold was the sticker itself.

I pushed on the door. The lock held for five seconds before snapping out of the frame.

The inner door was equipped to open on a signal from the apartments above. It was propped open with the broken end of a softball bat. I wondered whether the intercom and lock still worked and whether anyone cared.

From an open room down the hall a radio blared something about doing what you want and breaking my heart. Not a bad song for this building. I scuffed a newspaper aside and knocked on the door frame.

The man who appeared filled the frame from side to side but left about three feet of it free on top. I found myself looking down onto a bald head with ulcers on it. He looked up and frowned. Now, unfortunately, I could see his teeth. "Yeah?"

"You the manager?"

"Door says so." He looked around crossly for the door, found it to his left and jerked a gnawed thumbnail at it. "Whaddaya want?"

"To ask a few questions."

"Cop?" He put a lot of disgust into the word. These refined types often take offense that way.

"Nah. Private investigator." I flashed a photocopy of

my license and, incidentally, a ten-dollar bill. "One of your ex-boarders is a happy man."

"Happy how?" He was watching the ten with that puzzled expression a cat gets when he wants to swat but isn't sure yet. With a little effort I could probably get his whole head waving back and forth.

"Happy rich, is how. If you could find him, there might be something in it for you."

"How long ago was he here?" He hardly looked at me; Alexander Hamilton's picture, on the bill, was more attractive. Maybe I should have felt insulted.

"A year and a half ago. He roomed here last March and April. Stan Colfax." Now for the denial.

Instead I got a sneer. "That bum. I mighta known somebody'd come looking for him. He was nothing but grief."

"Is that right? When exactly did he move out?"

The ten's magic was fading. I'd mentioned somebody with a record. "I dunno. I heard about it from the old manager. I ain't had this job that long."

"Come off it." I leaned in. "You don't have a bed in here, and none of the mailboxes says 'Manager.' You're too cheap to hire anybody; you're the owner. You've been the owner, and you're dodging because you don't want law around here."

He just stared with red-rimmed eyes. He wasn't scared, and he wasn't mad. Sooner or later he'd be one or the other.

"Free country," he said finally.

"That's right. All of it's free. Some of it's cheap, too." I sighed and put the ten away. "The man could use the money. If you don't hate him, why not give him a break? Hell, he couldn't have got under your skin too far; he only lived here two months."

He spat in his own hall. "Two months? Two days."

I said, even though I knew the answer. "I heard he took

the apartment for two months. He must have paid two months' rent.''

''Sure. Once for the first of the month, one month in advance for damage deposit. I got to keep this place up.'' He might have meant it literally; the end of the hall looked like a couple of large jacks were in order.

So he'd told the cop that Colfax had been here two months, then kept the rent and the deposit. The cop, a novice, had bought it. Colfax wasn't likely to object from jail, particularly if he wanted to seem as if he'd been in town a while.

''Fine. Where'd he go?''

''Cops took him.'' He was puzzled. ''You need me to tell you that?'' That bothered him.

''Guess not. Thanks for your time.''

As I turned to leave, he said plaintively, ''What about the money?''

I didn't answer. He shouted at my back, ''I knew you was lying. Knew it alla time. Get outa here, you cheap bastard. I run a clean place.''

I stepped carefully over a Styrofoam burger package in the front hall and wondered where he ran it.

I put the accident report in a green-tabbed file (for active cases) and set it on my desk. I pulled out the journal from the same year and thumbed through it, listing names and checking them off against the files. We'd found Mr. Flanagan's wife; he punched me in the eye and we took him to small-claims court for our fee. Sara Pease never got her daughter back, but she never paid us, either. There were three names I didn't recognize except from Roy's conversation; all had closed files, one-day business and quick payments. Seth Barber had called off the search; I noted him down and and went on.

Three missing teenagers, two found. They always run to the IDS Plaza, where either the cops find them, or the wrong people do, and they end up prostitutes in New York City. Amazing, isn't it? Just like your mother warned you.

I noted all the stray phone calls, the crank messages or the cases that didn't pan out. Most were in my handwriting; Roy had figured that the junior partner should handle the irritating chores. I saw his point. Right now *I* wanted a junior partner.

And there it was, the last name in March, in Roy's handwriting: Emil Firebourne, R.R. 1, Belle View, Minn. Business confidential. Will call back. No note that he had. I must have been out to lunch that day, or busy on a case.

Belle View is a farm town, a county seat in a rural county. It would take some fast dodging for Emil Firebourne and Stanley Colfax not to know each other. I made a note and put it in the Cartley file.

And I noticed that my hands were shaking. On a normal day I would have taken Firebourne's call myself.

Chapter Four

Hamline and Macalester were tied. Equal numbers of their fans cheered the teams and booed the referees. The weather was crisp, clean and perfect.

Annie had gone to St. Kate's but had dated someone from Hamline. Or so she told me. She was cheering Macalester.

"Have a good week?" she said, too casually.

"Sure." I tried to think what else I could say without mentioning Roy.

Jon and I had learned a present address for Colfax from his parole officer. He was living in Belle View, in a house he could only afford because someone had helped him out. The parole officer hadn't said who. I badly wanted to know.

Firebourne was still alive in Belle View; when we knew more, we'd call on him. At Jon's office I listened in on the extension while Jon asked the local sheriff, an agreeable if not too eager ex-Marine named Josh Farrell, about Colfax.

"Nope. No trouble."

"None?"

"Not any more. He grew up here; you know that?"

"Sure." Jon caught himself and winced.

"How 'bout that. Casual call, y'say." Farrell sounded lazy, but that didn't make him dumb. "Care to talk?"

"Not by phone. We'll be down later in the month."

" 'We?' You don't make it easy not to ask."

"Sorry." Jon rubbed his eyes. Some laid-back county sheriff from a small town was turning him inside out without breathing hard. "You said 'not any more.' What was he into before cleaning up his act?"

"Oh, stuff like most of his family. Real outlaw types, they are. Drinking, reckless driving. Little vandalism. Burglary, maybe, but he never got caught, so you never heard me say that."

"Right. No problem. He sounds like a real mess. Traffic violations?"

"Not many. We warned him he could lose his license, and he got careful. For a while." Farrell sighed. "Damn shame a boy that talented couldn't stay straight."

"Always is. What talent?"

"Driving," He sounded surprised. "Never was a better boy around here on the stock circuit."

Jon stared at the phone. I mouthed something at him, then gave up. "Sorry to break in. Jon's a city boy; he wouldn't think to ask. What race was Stanley best at?"

After a silence the sheriff said quietly, "Something's up. I'll tell you when you come down."

I was even softer. "Say it. I think I can guess."

"You've got this far. Maybe you can. Other people cracked up, but Stan never even spun out, after his first year. Demolition Derby, with a couple of wins in the figure eight."

A chubby man wrapped in an army blanket shouted, "First and ten! Go, Mac!" and a couple of Hamline fans glared at him. At least he'd jarred my mind back to the game.

Annie said, "Any new cases come in?"

"What? No. Not really. Uh, I may have found Terry Selinoff. Or he's found me."

"That's a lead-in if I ever heard one. What happened?"

"I got a phone call last night at one A.M. Somebody yelled at me for three minutes in a foreign language, then slammed the phone down."

"Poor Nate. Did you understand anything?"

"One or two words."

"What were they?"

"I'd rather not say."

She laughed and put an arm around me. "That's what you get for doing business over the phone."

"Right." I leaned back and put my arm across her shoulders. It felt nice, even if I wasn't cold. Fall days like this were Minnesota's best. Maybe New England or Canada has autumns like this. I don't need to check.

I thought about what she'd said about phones, though. The date on the Belle View call from Firebourne had been wrong for it to have been from Roy's murderer. There was an odd note at the end of the journal, though: "Call, 12:30. No information. WCB."

Will Call Back. We'd neither of us left such empty entries before. If someone had arranged a secret meeting with Roy, Roy would have told me, possibly even asked me to tail him.

When I told Jon that, he looked thoughtful. "We know Roy was headed up north. There's no obvious connection to the Belle View call — hell, it's in the opposite direction — but there's no obvious connection to anything else, either. He didn't tell you where he was going, and he didn't have any private business there."

"You sure?"

"How can I be sure?"

"You can ask Edith Cartley."

"No." Jon had looked old enough in the last couple of years; now he looked haggard. "She won't know. If we find the man, maybe. Otherwise, forget it."

That was something to think about later. I watched the ball game in peace. At the end of it (Mac, 14-13, in the last ten seconds), Annie dropped me off at home when I explained that I had to run an errand.

"What errand? I thought I was buying you dinner tonight."

"Damn. Guess we'll have to have a third date."

"Don't pull that. We'll go out again, but I owe you a meal."

"Wish I could go, Annie. I really can't."

She asked, then broke off. Life was getting awkward.

She only stayed long enough to say hello to Marlowe. Like all cats, he decided to be difficult. Millions of people not to like in the Twin Cities, damn him, and he picked Annie. She left, I threw him outside, and I drove downtown.

I stuck my arm out the window and raised the antenna on the walkie-talkie. "Testing. Testing."

"Cut it out, Nate. You know they work." Jon's voice crackled. I got a strange echo; he was only ten feet away. I watched as he got into his beat-up Buick.

This was a stupid thing we were doing. At four o'clock on Saturday there wasn't much of a rush hour, but there was enough traffic to be risky. That was the point.

On Friday Jon and I had reviewed the accident report about twenty times. Roy had driven north on 35W to the point where it takes off north of 94. Colfax had roared down the first on-ramp past University, merged without looking and smashed Roy into the guardrail and back into the oncoming traffic. End of story. If Colfax's car had been tailing Roy's or if Colfax had been a little less drunk, the accident investigation might have been different.

Now it would be. I turned the key as Jon took off in front of me, going fast but not too fast. Was he giving me every chance? I thought the point was to make it hard.

I let a car slip between us, and I nearly rear-ended it at a yellow light on Ninth Street when Jon braked suddenly. That wasn't like Jon, either.

I stuck the walkie-talkie antenna back out. "What are you doing?" No answer. Jon was signaling his left turn already, and he started using the hand signal, then pulled his arm back. I realized with a sudden ache that he was driving as much like Roy as possible; Jon never drove cautiously, slowly, or timidly, and he had more faith in breaklights and blinkers than Roy ever had.

The sky was still absurdly blue, that rich dye it gets in early fall when the air is dry and things are never as clear again. What a great day. I wished I was on a picnic.

The bottle between my knees slipped. I swore and grabbed it. Bourbon slopped onto my trousers. Before the car had smelled; now it reeked.

We were crossing Chicago Avenue when the walkie-talkie sputtered again. "Make your move."

"Too early."

Jon said quietly, "He had a bigger car." I floored it, easing off as the passing gear kicked in. The car surged ahead in that half-hearted way most cars have these days.

Just for show, I passed Jon when he was behind a truck, then passed the truck before pulling in. I was maybe three blocks ahead of Jon, and I saw why he was driving like Roy. Even with a passing lane available there were two cars behind him; at that speed there always would be. If he lost control, some innocent bystander would knock him into the next world.

I pulled opposite the U. of M. medical complex. I remembered driving this stretch in blinding snow one

April, looking at the few lights in the buildings and thinking how isolated I was. Today the buildings looked almost cheerful in the sun, and I was surrounded by happy motorists enjoying their weekend. Terrific.

I had time as I crossed the river to look downstream at the Minnesota Avenue Bridge. At the U. we always heard stories about people jumping off; it got national attention a couple of years later when some poet named John Berryman jumped from it. From here it was just a great view.

I drove up the University Avenue exit. This was the tricky part. I held the bottle up and watched in the rearview mirror. Another car started up the ramp, slowed, then saw that my way was clear. He honked. What was wrong with me?

Jon appeared in my mirror, moving steadily along in the right lane. Now.

I tipped the bottle up, swallowing as much as I could in two gulps, then dropped the bottle and floored it. The car lurched; it was no '67 Chevy.

It was powerful enough. I swerved through the Fourth Street intersection, ignored shouts and screeching brakes, and picked up still more speed as I shot down the approach ramp. Matching Jon was no problem, even for an amateur.

My eyes watered from the bourbon, but I could see him just ahead; a little jockeying put me in position. Jon, naturally, moved into the left lane to let me merge. A VW Rabbit began pulling up beside him.

Almost frantically I whipped out of the merge lane and sent my car to within inches of Jon's fender — closer, in fact, than I'd wanted to. Behind me I heard nothing but brakes and horns. As I pulled back into my own lane I saw a flash of bright metal. We'd passed the point where Jon hit the guardrail. My car wasn't as powerful as Colfax's had been. Like I say, it was enough.

I pulled to the side of the road, shaking. John pulled in front of me. Unexpectedly, a third car stopped, and a man built like an oil drum hopped out and bounced up and down. "You stupid bastard! You stupid, stupid bastard!"

I mumbled, "Sorry," and wiped my eyes. They were still watering, and my stomach felt like hell.

He ran up to me, but smelled my shirt and my breath before he could hit me. "You're drunk!" he said unbelievingly. "What's wrong with you?"

I almost said I wasn't drunk, then realized it wouldn't be true much longer. "Look, I said I'm sorry."

"Sorry? Sorry? You nearly killed me, you know that?"

"Sure." Which was true, but shook him up.

Jon flashed his badge. "I'll take it from here."

The other man stared. "You okay, fella? I thought he'd —" He did a double take and grinned. "A cop. He almost killed a cop."

"Some guys have the luck." Jon turned me around. "Hands on the car." He frisked me quickly but thoroughly; I suppose it was too much of a habit for him to fake. I was glad I'd left my .38 at home. I wondered what the citizen would have thought if Jon had pulled that out of my suit.

"Need any help? A witness? Anything?" His voice was small and mean. "I want him brought to justice." He wanted me nailed.

"No, thanks. I'm a witness, too."

"I'll say. Jesus, you were almost a victim."

"Right. Thanks for your help. Could you move your car now? I can take it from here. 'You have the right to remain silent —' "

He mumbled until the bouncy man was back on the road. "Keep the hands up a second, Nate." The Rabbit disappeared. "Okay. Could you have got me?"

I lowered my hands. "Easy. I almost did by accident. Or I could have done it off that other car, if I didn't care how many people I took with you. Jon, we shouldn't have done this. Someone might have bought it."

"We had to know."

"Nobody needs to know that badly. Sure, I could've done it. A Demo Derby driver wouldn't have any trouble at all. Now what?"

"The blood test. Think you'll pass?"

I coughed. "No way." Later it turned out I had more bourbon in me than Colfax had. I also had a whopping, sick-making hangover. "Jon, it's possible. It's starting to seem likely. Now what?"

"We drive back to the station —"

I looked dizzily back at the highway and all but wailed, "I can't drive like this!"

That stopped him short. "Right. Listen, leave your flashers on and I'll send someone back for the car. Hope no one hits it."

"Yeah," I said numbly. "This is a bad place. Merging traffic." I got in his car, feeling sick and wobbly and unhappy. My car was sitting in a bad place. We'd proved that our best friend's death could have been intentional.

And in the interests of justice we'd risked the lives of perfect strangers while we rehearsed a murder.

Chapter Five

Want to hear the entirety of the Darnell Case? At ten-thirty Monday morning a woman named Janet Darnell walked into my office and cried for ten minutes, saying her daughter Helen had run off with a middle-aged man and she, Janet, would pay five hundred dollars to get her back. I said, "Cash, get it now, and I won't work on anything else, including sleep, till she's found."

She went for the money, leaving me with a picture of a dark-haired, dark-eyed thirteen-year-old with no more obvious intelligence than a seedless grape. Mrs. Darnell had been gone ten minutes when her daughter came in, waving a wad of grubby ones and fives and asking for help. I told her to keep her money. What was wrong?

After five more minutes of Darnell tears, she told me that her stepfather, H. Clarence Darnell, had been making passes at her and she couldn't stand it any more. So much for Mrs. Darnell's theory.

I told her I'd do what I could, treated her to a less-than-modest lunch, and took her to talk to a social worker. That was rough, but fast. On the way out I called Mrs. Darnell, and at my office she and Helen cried a duet. I took the reward, probably under less protest than I should have made, since the five hundred came from the collected savings of H. Clarence Darnell — and the hell with him.

I called Annie. She listened, then said flatly, "That's a pretty flip way to talk about a girl's life being blown apart."

"I know."

"So?"

"So what can I do for her, anyway?"

"Is that why you called me? You're angry, aren't you?"

"Not half as mad as H. Clarence will be when he checks his balance and asks where the money went."

"So that's some kind of revenge."

"I wanted to do something. Taking her to lunch wasn't enough."

"You took her to get help. You did what you could. Why act like you don't care, though?"

"I don't know."

"Because you're angry."

I thought. "You're right. I'm angry. And I wanted to talk. Thanks for listening. What do you get out of this?"

"Out of what?"

"Out of, uh, seeing me."

"There has to be a better phrase for it; I sound like a window peeker. I get a work break. Call you later in the week. In the meantime, give up on acting like you don't care. You think you're as tough as your damn cat."

"Nobody's as tough as my damn cat."

She hung up. I made tea and wondered how soon she'd call.

I didn't spend my whole day waiting, though, and I was caught off guard when, at ten to six, my phone rang just as I took a broiling pan with two pork chops out of the oven.

I dragged Marlowe over to the phone and held onto his collar. "Hello?"

"Nate." Annie sounded terrible. "I don't even know how to say this."

"You okay?" I almost let go of Marlowe, but tightened my hold when he began struggling. He looked longingly at the broiling pan. "I can be there in —"

"No, no, I'm fine. Thanks, though." She sounded even worse. "Nate, I've been trying to track down the two men who set up Roy Cartley."

"And?" Marlowe squeaked like a stuffed toy. I let go. I hadn't realized I'd tightened my grip.

"Oh, God, Nate, I found them, and —"

"How? Where are you? Are you — ?"

"I'm fine." Her voice had a edge in it. "I told you that. And my finding them would have been just luck, except for one thing. I followed your friend and saw him with them."

I was lost. "What friend? Who? They're after a friend of mine?"

"They're not after him. They work for him. Jon Pederson. He knew about the whole thing before we ever went to him. He set up your partner."

I watched Marlowe leaping onto the formica with a half-inch to spare, flipping a hot pork chop off the stove, then dropping beside it and pulling it daintily into the dining room. I didn't feel like doing anything. "You're wrong."

"Nate, I saw him."

"You've got to be wrong."

"Nate, I didn't want to tell you, but I had to. I saw him. This afternoon, after you and I talked."

"Why are you doing this? Why do you keep telling me things like this?" My head hurt suddenly, a sharp pain in the temples; I knew it was with me for the night. "I like you. Why are you making that hard?"

"I can't help it." She started to say something else, but stopped.

I didn't care. I was barely listening. "Not Jon. You're wrong."

"I have proof. A Polaroid shot. I think he saw me. We can't meet in my place or yours; can you be at Minnehaha Creek below First Street in thirty minutes?"

"Why don't we —"

"There, or nowhere. I'm spooked, Nate. This is your world, not mine."

What could I do? I went. Marlowe didn't look up from his chop.

The drive is a blank. I know I headed south and didn't hit anybody; other than that I couldn't tell you a thing. I was thinking about Saturdays, two years ago, when Roy would call Jon up if we were working and he'd meet us in the office for lunch and growl at us. We'd play clubs for a penny a point. Win or lose, Jon always claimed we cheated.

I got out of the car after parking below the overpass and stepped into the trees. Annie was there. I didn't bother saying hello. "Show me the picture."

She didn't look scared, merely sick — that worn-down misery when you're ashamed of yourself and of everyone around you. "Nate, I'm sorry. This wasn't my idea." She swallowed. "I'm always apologizing to you —"

There was a scuffle in the first fallen leaves as Jon stepped from behind a maple. He said without looking at me, "Now you know how someone could keep Roy from telling you about a call. Not the only way, just the easiest."

I didn't get it. He added, "You didn't call to check with me, did you? Anything less and you would have."

What could I say? I kicked at the leaves and wouldn't look at either of them. Jon had a beautiful red maple leaf stuck on top of his shoe; somehow he hadn't even crumpled it. I stared at it and said, "That's vicious."

I'm surprised either of them heard me, but Jon nodded. "It is. But whatever they said about you, Roy wouldn't believe it. He felt obliged to check. That's all."

" 'Obliged to' — what do you think it was?''

"Who knows? Could be almost anything.'' He added, gently, "Probably something rough, though. Sorry.''

I still wasn't feeling talkative. "Why Annie?''

Now it was Jon's turn to look at fallen leaves. "Be reasonable. There's no investigation, officially; who else could I ask?''

Annie came over and took my hand. That was nice of her, but I barely noticed. One side of her mouth smiled, a very little. "I make a great friend, don't I?''

I squeezed her hand, but didn't feel any better. Roy had died checking whether I was a criminal. Jon had tricked me through Annie, all to prove a point that hurt me badly. "Don't worry about it.'' My voice wasn't normal just yet. "Apparently, that's what friends are for.''

Chapter Six

Around us it was still surprisingly green, fostered by rain and warm weather. Usually this late in the season Minnesota has what interior decorators call earth tones: the light brown of corn stalks and chaff, the chocolate of underbrush and the rich black of midwestern plowed land. Some day soon fall plowing would take all this away; the topsoil would drift, and the green would fade. For now, though, it was the richest color imaginable, and the loveliest.

Jon stretched. "Neck gets tired on long drives."

"Squad car teams drive longer."

"I wouldn't know any more." But he said it wistfully; Jon was still no good at delegating hard work. It had taken him until Thursday to get his desk clean enough to join me.

"Want me to take over?"

"You kidding? With my luck we'd run into that guy that thinks I busted you."

"Look, it's my car. I'll bet you were a lousy passenger on patrol."

"You're right." He put a hand behind his neck. There wasn't much to rub besides bone and muscle. "You should get cruise control."

"You love speeding too much." He slowed down. "You know where to turn?"

"Farrell told me. Can't miss it."

Somewhere between ROAD HAZARDOUS WHEN WET and NO TRESPASSING: SURVIVORS WILL BE PROSECUTED, I said, "Jon? Why aren't we going to see Emil yet?"

"We'll go see him when we have enough evidence."

"Evidence of what?" He didn't answer. "Jon, you're not trying to make a collar. Down here, you're not even a cop."

He hit the brakes and stared at me. "When I see Firebourne, I want him to know that I know he's guilty. I don't want him to have any chance of stalling me and running. When I see him, it all ends."

"In an arrest," I said flatly.

"Check those damn directions. We're still lost." I gave up.

Finally we came to a hand-lettered sign: "Floyd Crossing." We bumped over the diagonal filler where the crossing used to be. The tracks had been taken out recently; you could see the bare, abandoned right of way to the north and south, scarred and unnatural. On the far side of the tracks at an elbow bend in the road were a couple of frame houses with windbreaks. Welcome to Floyd Crossing.

Jon pulled in at the mailbox that said "Colfax." He shut the car off and stared. "Quite a step up." I nodded.

You couldn't say Colfax had taste, but he had time. By the blue-and-white birdbath there was a spotted plaster mushroom with a frog lounging on it. Further up was a scale-model Dutch windmill; the breeze turned the blades slowly this morning. By the front steps was a jockey with a lantern. At least the jockey was painted white. There was more of the same around to the side, if you can call any of it "the same." At the back were three wooden beehives.

Jon knocked, then squinted at the woodwork thought-fully. "Nice paint job. Think he'd do my place?"

"Why not?" I pointed to where he'd scratched his initials and the date in the front steps. "He likes the work."

The door opened. I waited for my blood pressure to go up, for Jon to grab Colfax by the collar and ask who the hell he thought he was, killing Roy.

Nothing happened. We both stared at a tousled, good-natured twenty-five-year-old carrying his coffee. "If you're not selling something, you're sure as shoot lost. Can I help you?" He waved the mug apologetically, even though he hadn't done anything.

While Jon closed his mouth, I said, "Sorry to come by so early —"

"Early?" He laughed. "I been up four hours. Can't sleep. I just hold back drinkin' coffee till ten; I'm tryin' to learn to sleep late. Here, c'mon in."

He held open the freshly varnished door, and we slipped inside the new aluminum storm door on to his brand-new entryway all-weather carpet.

Jon said softly, "Try chopping wood."

"Huh?"

"Most cons when they get out can't sleep late. Some of them can't stay awake past lights-out. Friend of mine bought four cords of wood, chopped it an hour before sunset. He'd fall asleep after dinner, snooze for an hour or so. That broke his sleeping patterns; you can't nap after meals in jail." Jon shrugged. "Once you've licked one habit, the rest are easier."

The good nature was half gone. "What's this about?"

On cue I handed him a card an insurance agent had given me once. It didn't have a name on it. "Nathan Phillips." No handshake; he wouldn't offer, yet. "I investigate insurance work for these people." I work my way into lying a little at a time.

He nodded. "You're way late. I been in. I did my time.

It's over." And it had left a few scars; he reached casually behind the inside door.

"You didn't let me finish. I'm doing a follow-up. Your answers will be confidential —" That shot any chance we had at getting evidence, but so did Jon's presence. "And they would greatly help other policy holders." I coughed. "Perhaps even people like yourself, who have an accident record."

He looked at both of us without saying anything. Jon was rubbing his back, just above the pocket where he'd slipped his gun. If Colfax had his hand on a gun, it wouldn't even be close.

Then Colfax pulled his hand back, shrugging. "Okay. C'mon in." We wiped our feet.

"Sit down." The formica kitchen table, scarred but clean, was the oldest thing we'd seen so far. "Coffee?"

"Thanks." Jon sipped it carefully, even though we'd both watched Colfax pour. "Most of this isn't going to be about the accident."

"That's good. 'Cause I don't wanna talk about it." He moved around jerkily, making the tea I'd asked for instead of coffee. "I feel bad, and all, but it's over. My time's over. I gotta put my life back together."

Jon nodded. "That's what we need to know." I was surprised, but didn't show it. Earlier, we'd rehearsed a whole good-cop, bad-cop scenario. "Nathan, why don't you take out your pad?"

I took. "I guess you now who's boss here, Mr. Colfax." That got a smile.

Jon frowned at me. To Colfax he said, "How long have you been out of prison?"

"Couple months. You can look that up."

"Close enough. Have you been inclined to drink heavily?"

"Nope. I keep some, but I don't touch it much." He added defensively, "Never did. Just a real bender once in a while." He sounded wistful. "I kinda don't like it now."

"You'd be surprised how many of our interviewees say that," I put in. Very surprised; he was the only one.

"Don't say anything that might influence him, Nate. It prejudices the results." Jon was good at this. I was still doing the lying for both of us, but Jon was convincing.

"Have people behaved differently toward you in any way since your release — friends, family, business acquaintances?" Nice, Jon. "Business" slid in so smoothly it hardly bumped.

Colfax shrugged. "They can't help it. They think they're being nice, but they ain't. Even Ma looks at me different; half of her says she's glad I'm out and half says where'd she go wrong. You learn to ignore it."

"Friends? Thanks." I took the cup.

"Varies. Some are pretty good. Some pretend nothing's changed, but that won't work." He stared into his coffee. "The worst are the ones who feel so damn good about themselves for talking to you. Them you want to hit. 'Course, I don't," he added hastily. "But I hate the way they look at you, and talk like you're a retarded kid and didn't know any better."

"And what about business acquaintances?" I kept my head down, staring at the pad, and sipped my tea.

He took so long that I risked looking up. He stared into my eyes and finally said defensively, "The truth? I don't have any. What I did before was drive truck for construction; they don't want me. I see the other drivers, but they're scared to socialize, seeing's what we mostly did before was drink together. I don't have a job. Pretty soon I got to start looking."

"It's good that you can take some time," Jon said gently, and I almost thought he meant it. "Most ex-cons go straight from prison routine to jobs, and it confuses them — the schedules are totally different. It takes a while just to get used to opening windows."

Colfax grinned. "Don't I know it. First thing every morning I open my own door. The first couple days my stomach knotted up before I tried it, and I waited for alarms to go off. Habit's a hell of a thing. More coffee?"

"Thanks. Nate, can you think of anything I haven't covered?"

"Uh, there's material on living expenses. That is, if Mr. Colfax is willing to discuss it." I refilled my teacup.

"Right." Jon tapped the side of his cup with his index finger. "You don't have to answer any of these questions, Mr. Colfax, but if you do, let me repeat, your replies will be confidential."

"Okay. I may not answer." Colfax looked wary, and his right arm tensed. I was willing to bet that was a prison reflex. God, he looked strong.

"Thanks for letting me ask. Since your release, have you received cash or loans from family?"

"A little from Ma, that's it. She doesn't have much. She won't let me pay her back, either."

Jon smiled briefly. So help me God, I looked more like a cop than he did. "Parents can be like that. What about friends?"

"Friends, right. Al Cerwinske bought me a load of groceries when I moved in, and Brenda Anderson — she went with me back when she was single — bought me a lamp; but there hasn't been much of that. Couple people have had me to dinner."

This time Jon asked the obvious. "Has someone you used to work with helped you, or have you been living off savings until you find a job?"

"Yeah, well, mostly savings. Listen, I'm not sure I want to answer any more questions."

I had two names, aside from his mother's. Some interrogation. We shook hands and thanked him.

I stopped on the front lawn. "You've got a great collection here. How long did it take you?"

"Aren't they terrific?" He grinned again. "I got all of those since I got out. Mostly at yard sales; I painted 'em all myself."

That explained the colors. "I think they look great. Your landlord — what does he think? Landlords can be funny —"

"He never gives me any trouble." The grin was wider, and I wondered if I'd missed something.

Jon, by the car, said, "You know, that was the only question left."

"What?"

"Your landlord. Does he know your record, did he make any special lease conditions, does he treat you differently than he would another tenant?"

The grin was gone. "He doesn't do any of that. And he knows. Listen I better get back to work."

"Right. Thanks for your time." I glanced at the back. "Those beehives make me nervous. I hate getting stung."

He laughed. "*You* hate it? I'm allergic."

"You're kidding."

"Nope. Swell up like a balloon. Doctor says it's a histamine reaction. If my throat goes shut, I'll die and no mistake." In the sunlight we could see bees circling the wooden boxes before doing whatever bees do while they're out.

"Then why keep them?"

Colfax said lazily, "I ain't scared." For the first time I could see the side that got him in trouble, the part that didn't care enough or think enough to avoid grief. I stopped liking him, without realizing that I'd started. "I wear gear, most of the time. Life's a risk, is all."

On the way out the driveway we slowed, and I twisted the side-mirror so I could see Colfax. He was watching us, then staring at the house down the road.

"Left?" I said to Jon.

"Yah. Up the road a mile, then to the left again."

With me driving it took us five minutes to get to the neighboring house. Jon would have taken three. He chewed me out for getting to the car keys first. We checked the name on the mailbox: Brian Frees. Good German name, I guessed. Compared to Colfax's house, this one was a bastion of good taste: near the grape arbor there was an A-frame birdhouse with trim in the same white as the siding; no lawn statuary at all.

Brian Frees was more subtle, too. He took two rings to get to the door, and he was wearing a cardigan and solid-color slacks. An awful lot of men his age opted for plaid trousers; it was a relief to walk to a farm door and not greet what looked like an escaped golfer. He scratched his balding head, nodded genially to the two of us over black-rimmed glasses and said, "Help ya?"

"We're making a survey." I flashed my card. "Could we ask you a few questions, Mr. Frees?"

"Come right in." He wasn't surprised enough; Stan had been on the phone.

This time we declined coffee. Jon's stomach is made of iron, but I get jumpy.

"How did you know my name?"

Other than your mailbox? But Jon replied, in one of his oblique lies, "We've been interviewing one of your tenants, a Mr. Colfax —"

"Yah, yah. He in trouble?" He peered concernedly at us, and I felt ashamed.

"Oh, no. We simply interviewed him for information on . . . claimants and persons involved in accidents." Jon gave the phoniest smile possible. "We'd like to ask a few questions about him."

"Yah, well, that's not right, is it?"

"You're free to refuse, sir," That was bait: he could only learn the next question by answering the last one.

"Well, okay." He sat with his arms folded, waiting. That way he didn't look quite so pot-bellied.

Jon took out his own glasses and adjusted them, looking at a sheet that actually had notes on it. "When you rented to Mr. Colfax, did you know his background?"

"You mean about his being in jail? Yah, sure. Rest of

his background, too." He shrugged without unfolding his arms. "I've known his family a long time."

I broke in, "Is that why you rented to him?" Jon frowned at me, but I wanted to see if Frees took the bait.

"Sure. I guess. Better than renting to strangers."

"Then the other people who offered to rent that house were strangers?"

Frees looked uncomfortable. "Well, sure. Leastways, I knew Stan's family better."

"I see." Jon looked down at his sheet, a not-so-subtle way of shutting me up. "I understand that Mr. Colfax is unemployed."

"Not exactly."

"I didn't catch that," Jon said deadpan.

" 'Not exactly.' See, I'm gonna hire him, but he wants to rest first. Jail's pretty hard on people, I guess." The arms were still folded, but Frees was staring everywhere but at our eyes.

I opened my mouth; on a look from Jon I shut it. Jon said, "That's very commendable, sir," a bit too smoothly. "Still, we can't help wondering where his rent money is coming from, and what he used for his deposit."

"I think maybe he had some money saved up from his stock-car days. He won some prizes, and he had a job back then. Maybe his mom helped out. Gee, I don't know. Is it important?" He stared at us anxiously.

"Not really, sir. We just like to gather background on our respondents. All of your answers will be kept confidential." Whatever that meant.

"Yah, well, okay. But I think that's all I better say, all right?" He looked from one of us to the other, his forehead puckered. "Stan, he's a good boy that made a mistake, that's all. One mistake. Can you be so hard on a guy for one mistake?" The answer seemed to mean a lot to him.

I smiled brightly at him. "Not us. We're hoping this

survey will change insurance rates for convicted drunk drivers. Thank you for your time." I sounded like a stewardess at the end of a flight. Frees shook hands, but he didn't follow us out.

Halfway to town I said, "Jon, he's lying."

"I know. He's too nervous."

"Not just that. Hardly anybody rents a farmhouse to strangers unless it's near a college. Mostly what you get is locals. Other folks rent in town." All this country time was taking me back to the way I used to talk.

Jon swore softly. "We'd better look into him."

"Sure. Courthouse, sheriff's office —"

"So much for the small-town boy. Newspaper office."

"What?"

"Check the ads for the time Colfax got out. If Frees's rental house wasn't advertised then, we know he's lying."

Right. And faster than starting with plat books and working forward.

In the end, we did go to the courthouse. Colfax's house hadn't been advertised for rent, but I found a for-sale ad from a month before he was paroled that sounded familiar. We called, pretending we'd seen a back issue and asking if the house was still for sale. Sure enough, Frees had bought it. The realty office offered us four more places before we got off the phone; these days the market for farmhouses was glutted.

At the courthouse we confirmed the transaction and the price, then rechecked the newspapers and confirmed something the realtor had said: Frees could have bought any number of cheaper houses if he hadn't wanted Colfax close enough to keep an eye on him. Frees hadn't needed to be sneaky. Realtors these days would sell to one-eyed men with knives, and Frees was a respectable local.

At the Crystal Café we had a late lunch. I munched on my BLT, not thinking about murder or Roy. "Now what?"

Jon pushed French fries around his plate. "We see Frees again. Good-cop and bad-cop this time. We call him first."

"Gives him time to run."

"Wastes a trip if he's out. Question is, do we call the sheriff?" He smothered a fry in ketchup, popped it in his mouth, and answered his own question. "No."

"Don't talk with your mouth full. Think that's smart, Jon?"

"It's no problem. We're not making a collar, and we don't know enough yet."

That might have been true of Firebourne; I didn't think it was of Frees. Still, I didn't push him. Jon was still smarting over the mistake he'd made investigating Roy's death the first time.

We tossed for who would call Frees — I won, but Jon called anyway. "Finish up." I gulped and we left.

I navigated again. "Take the blacktop north. Quicker this way."

"You sure?"

"Almost. What did Frees say?" Jon was driving even faster than usual; he hit sixty almost before the northern town limits sign.

Jon looked worried. "He said fine, and did I mind if Colfax was there. Said Colfax was over taking care of a bee swarm for him."

"Is that a problem?"

"Might be. Check the glovey, okay?" The glove compartment had Jon's gun and a box of cartridges. I checked the gun — Jon always unloads it when he doesn't need it — reloaded, put the safety on and laid it beside him. Then I did the same for mine. "Extra cartridges?"

"Yep." Now I understood the speed. He wanted to arrive before Colfax and Frees expected us. "If they're inside, we split up. I didn't tell him you were coming."

"I'll take back door. Uh, Jon?"

"Mmmm." He was checking the safety himself. Careful man.

"We are taking Colfax alive, right?"

He turned, startled. "Of course."

"Just wanted to make sure. You don't usually plan fire fights."

He looked at the road as we turned east, then back at me. "Nate, this Colfax is a life taker. Odds on, Frees is the man who hired him. I want them alive and without gunfire if I can, but I won't weep over either of them."

"Right." And I realized, sickeningly, that Jon was used to calling in backup. "No radio in this car."

"Huh? Oh. If we can't handle it, we back out. Fast. Maybe we should have called Farrell."

"We could still —"

"Too late now." He whipped to a stop up the road from Frees's property. The windbreak was between us and the house. "I'll walk up the drive. You —"

"I'll cut along the fencerow. I'm a farm boy, remember?"

"You keep telling me." Jon put his gun in his pocket. "You carry your gun out, Nate. I didn't drag you here to get you shot while you tear your coat up."

I thought I'd brought him. "Right." I dropped into the ditch and went over the fence as low as possible. My pants picked up some burrs, but I didn't care.

I quit following orders when I hit the windbreak. I moved from trunk to trunk until I was even with the front of the house. Jon had barely reached the mailbox. Probably he'd been checking the front windows.

I pressed flat against a tree trunk on the side opposite Jon, holding my gun high with the safety off. He was nonchalantly strolling to the front door, hand near but not in his pocket. One good shot from the windows would knock him back a foot before he could fire. He looked as brave as hell. I felt sick.

I tensed as the door opened. Frees stepped out. "Hiya. Didn't hear you pull in." His hands were empty.

"Didn't want to block your driveway." Jon didn't seem to relax, but I unbent for both of us. "There's something I'd better tell you, Mr. Frees: I'm a policeman."

Right. That was the other reason he wanted to hit up Frees alone: no lies and no complications.

Frees said, "Is that right?"

Jon smiled. "I guess I didn't surprise you." He pulled his badge out. "I have some questions for you and for Mr. Colfax —"

"Sure." But he didn't move.

Jon didn't like that. He looked this way and that, up at the second story, over toward me. "Where's —"

"Colfax?" Frees grinned. "He's catchin' a swarm of bees for me. Like I said on the phone. Waiting out back."

Jon's face dropped. I could have kicked myself. Colfax could be edging up either side of the house, and I couldn't be sure of stopping him now. So much for thinking for myself. I sprinted.

I realized dimly that Jon was running to the back, too. "Mr. Colfax?" He was shouting. That was crazy.

Oh. No it wasn't: Jon was drawing Colfax's fire, in case I was back there. I sprinted harder, gun behind me but ready.

I broke from the trees and looked in all directions. Nobody. Colfax was hidden, ready. I was an open target.

Then I saw him. I hadn't been looking for someone lying down, arms sprawled. His jacket had a dark stain over the chest, but neither Jon nor I had fired yet.

Then his hand moved, feebly.

Chapter Seven

I made it to him in ten seconds, most of it spent thinking about CPR and wondering if I remembered enough to help instead of kill him. He didn't appear to be breathing, and his right arm, flung across his chest, looked as though he was clutching at his heart. The stain on his plaid jacket was huge. I couldn't imagine that much blood drying so quickly. I knelt beside him, then pulled back.

Jon, catching up, said, "What the hell?" He touched Colfax's chest. "Christ."

"You two hold up." We whirled as Frees dashed into and out of a shed. He was carrying something and pulling on gloves at the same time.

We rocked on our heels by Colfax, trying to figure out what to do, until Frees came up. He poked the jacket with a gloved hand. "Oh, my. Clear down his chest. Swarm started dropping."

They had dropped over Colfax like tar, flowing over his collar onto his bare neck. Colfax hadn't even buttoned the jacket. Now it was just a wrapper for bees and a dying man.

I knelt down twice more, trying to get close. The second time I felt a sting at the back of my neck and jumped back six feet. The branch above me still had half the swarm on it.

Frees handed Jon and me rubber gloves. "Put 'em on." He ducked to one side of the overhanging branch with exaggerated care, opened the jacket and, with his own gloved hands, scooped masses of the bees into the pail beside him. Most of them stayed where he put them.

After a moment, Jon and I did the same. Through the fingers of the gloves you could feel the gobbets of bees crawling, shifting, clinging to each other and stinging futilely. The buzzing made me sweat, and I remembered something from when I was a boy about bees hating sweat. I couldn't remember if it was true or not. The back of my neck was swelling.

"Christ." I looked across at Jon; he was sweating, too. He must have been imagining it: Colfax strolling under that branch, peering up to see how best to gather in the swarm. Probably he'd reached up in that damn loose coat. A bee dropped off and inside it, stinging. Maybe two or three, and he'd passed out. Left unattended, even those few stings could do him in, but he'd fallen right under the branch. Another bee dropped — then another couple — then a few hundred more . . .

Frees said unsteadily, "That's most of 'em." He put a board over the bucket. "A couple pounds of bees. Drag him out from under, and we'll brush him off."

Jon and I stared at each other. We were so used to not moving victims, we'd never thought to pull him to a safer spot.

I grabbed Colfax under the armpits and heaved; the buzzing had me so keyed up that I tugged him four or five feet in one haul. His flesh felt puffed and oddly infirm to me. On my next pull, my hands slipped, and I pinched one of his swollen biceps. Colfax sat up with a terrible cry, and I fell over.

He turned toward where I sprawled, but I don't think he saw me. "Thirsty." He tried to turn his head, but his neck was too puffed. "Ah, God, am I thirsty." Under his own power he stood up, not noticing when Jon grabbed under one arm and Frees under the other. "The kitchen."

"Lie down," Jon said weakly, but I don't think Colfax heard. Probably the rush of blood in his own ears drowned out even the hum of the swarm. Why his windpipe wasn't swollen shut was beyond me. He shook free, crying aloud when Jon and Frees tried to restrain him, then stumbled toward the house.

What could we do? Touch him and he might have a heart attack. I ran ahead to call an ambulance, and the other two walked on either side of Colfax, spotting him.

His fingers slipped on the screen door; they were too puffed to bend. Frees caught and held it, wincing as it smacked his own stung fingers. He kicked the inside door open. Colfax walked the steps stiff-legged, breathing in short bursts. He was having a massive histamine reaction. He'd need oxygen soon, but it wouldn't save him.

"They say five minutes," I called from the phone. "Keep him lying down, treat for shock —"

"Yeah, sure." Jon slumped defeatedly in a kitchen chair as Colfax felt his way along the kitchen counter, squinting at the sink as though it was ten miles away. Frees watched all three of us, agony in his eyes.

Colfax turned the water on with the heel of his right hand. Holding a glass with two hands he filled it, bending over it almost reverently. Now his forehead and eyes were darkening like a huge bruise. He carried the glass to the table; none of us dared to grab it from him. It was like some strange blackmail — we couldn't help him without putting him in agony.

He slumped into a chair and peered from under massive eyebrows at the water. "God, that looks good," he said, simply and clearly.

Then he died, so easily and quickly that none of us noticed.

Fifteen seconds later, Jon pulled Colfax's unresisting body to the floor and pumped methodically but powerfully at his chest. I knelt on the other side, braced to pinch the nose that was swollen shut anyway and put my lips over Colfax's distorted mouth. The first time was the worst; I was half afraid what it might feel like.

Jon said, in rhythm with the count, "Airway okay? Seven, eight . . ."

"Fine." I wouldn't have been surprised if it had been swollen shut. Colfax's heart must have given out first. I puffed air into his lungs again. No reaction. His skin felt pebbly under my hands.

Jon and I traded places twice before the ambulance arrived. Two men in their twenties took over without batting an eye and shipped Colfax to the hospital. Later I heard that he'd been pronounced D.O.A.

Frees, Jon and I watched them go. Jon touched a couple of stings on his cheek, probably for the sake of feeling something besides numb. He said without looking at Frees, "Got any baking soda?"

Frees was already under the sink. "We all need it, I bet. Damn, what a sorry way to go."

I waited patiently for my turn with the paste Frees made. "What do you think he felt?"

"Nothing much." But Jon shivered as he said it. "After the first few stings he must've passed out. You saw that."

Frees rubbed his own arms down. "Hope you're right." He picked up the glass of water gingerly, as though it contained something deadly. "You two want a drink?"

Jon recoiled, then realized about the same time I did that he hadn't meant the water. "No, thanks." I could have used one, but shook my head; Jon probably had a good reason for refusing. Jon added, "We ought to get downtown, talk to the sheriff."

"Downtown? Oh, right." Small-town people don't make much out of going downtown. "Guess they oughta hear. Well, thanks for all you did." He held open the door gingerly; one of his fingers had been stung. "Wish it had turned out better."

"Thanks." Jon gave me a funny look when I said it; I tried to sound more sincere. "Listen, I'm sorry —"

"Nothin' you did. Hope things work out for you down here." He let the door swing shut and he turned away immediately.

At the car Jon said, "You okay?"

"Couple stings, is all. I —"

"Bullcrap." Country was making Jon more colorful. "Thinkin' of your father?"

"A little." Dad's first heart-attack had been scary enough, but it was mild compared to this. "Other things are bothering me."

"Frees?" He jerked his head toward the house wincing as his coat rubbed one of the bee stings. "Sure, you bet. Has to be a setup. No way to prove it, though."

"Terrific." I sat back carefully. "Do we talk to Firebourne?"

"Not yet. We talk to the sheriff, then drive back to the Twin Cities and nurse our wounds — what's wrong?"

"Unh. Shouldn't have sat up like that." I automatically rubbed my neck, then wished I hadn't. "But we've got our evidence. I don't know how I missed it. God, we're idiots."

"Spit it out." But he was intrigued. "I can't think of a thing."

"It's circumstantial, but it's a start. Remember Frees's trouble with the door?"

"Sure. Helluva bump on his ring finger, too. So?" Then Jon sat up. "And he —"

"Right. And the whole time we saw him beside the body, he was wearing gloves."

Chapter Eight

Sheriff Josh Farrell stood maybe six foot three, but it was hard to notice. Sideways across the navel he was maybe two and a half feet, with one of the most prodigious beer bellies I've ever seen. While we were there he petted a melancholy looking elderly beagle several times, calling it "Daisy dog." He looked powerful, but I couldn't imagine him running after anyone.

Still, he looked formidable. "Then what'd you do?"

Jon said listlessly, "We went back."

"To Frees?" Farrell's voice, deep enough on the phone, seemed to rumble up from his belly. Daisy growled.

"Yessir."

"You went back. You talked to him." Farrell put his hand, thumb and forefinger extended, across his forehead. "I hope you won't mind when I come up to Minneapolis and talk to suspects just ahead of you. What'd you say?" He swung around to me.

I'd been hoping he wouldn't, except that Jon needed a relief pitcher. "We pointed out that the swarm seemed pretty coincidental. We also pointed out that we knew he'd been stung some time before we found Colfax. He admitted borrowing Colfax's bee jacket and also that he knew Colfax was both reckless and allergic.''

"Covered the ground, didn't you? Real nice, giving him practice before any official questions.'' I wasn't sure Farrell would have come up with our questions; still, he had a point. "And did he answer?''

"It took a minute, but yes, he did. He said he couldn't tell bees what to do. He'd borrowed the jacket some time back, but he didn't feel competent to handle a swarm. He pointed out that when he tried he got stung, and that's why he called Colfax.''

Farrell turned to Jon. "What does a seasoned pro like you think of his answers?''

Farrell was only half sarcastic; Jon winced anyway. "I thought he explained too much. You don't call in a hotshot just because you got stung if you raise bees. If you do call him, you think to loan him his own jacket; chances are Colfax asked for it, and Frees pretended he'd loaned it to someone else. And I'm no farm boy, but I bet you can make bees swarm.''

Farrell nodded. "I wish to hell you'd had me out there, so life was nice and official. But you did a fine job. You're like Daisy dog, here: born sniffers. I might not have done as good.'' That didn't surprise me, and it didn't cheer Jon up.

Farrell pulled a battered book off his desk. "Librarian dropped this off when I called. Aren't small towns grand? Lemme read you some stuff.'' He turned to a page marked with a torn corner of newspaper and read aloud:

" 'In any case' — I'm skipping a lot — 'there is less tendency to swarm in late summer or early fall.' They say it happens sometimes. 'By noting the advancement of the queen cells it is often possible to predict on what day the swarm will issue.' So he could know when it was gonna happen.

"Here's the capper: 'Following is a summary of some of the most important swarm-preventive measures.' And here's a couple of them: 'Providing Abundant Ventilation.' 'Giving Shade.' You were too busy to check for airholes, but I bet you noticed that Frees's hives were in the sun, right? Thought so. I bet if you walked around his back yard you'd find the squares of bare ground from where he'd moved those hives." He read again. " 'Barrier of Sealed Honey Around the Brood Nest.' Well, that'd be easy to break.

"Lessee . . . a lot of these others just talking about providing enough room for the bees, which I'll guess he didn't. There's something here about 'Destroying Queen Cells,' which I'll guess he didn't do. This took some planning ahead, didn't it? He couldn't be sure exactly when they'd swarm, but he could make sure they did, and he could call Colfax the moment it happened. At that, the timing was pretty close, you two showing up and all."

He held the book open, like a deacon holds Scriptures, at arm's length in front of the listeners. "You've heard the word, Brother Pederson. Now, I could go to that farm tomorrow with a search warrant and a bee expert, and I could find Colfax's jacket and a load of handling equipment, and what do you think it would prove?"

We didn't answer. What was the use?

"Not a jeezly thing!" he roared, and slammed the book so hard the clipping blew two feet up in the air. "Quiet, Daisy! We could say anything we wanted about why he had it, and it wouldn't be good enough. Because, God damnit, you're never going to convince a Gordon County jury that you can premeditatedly honeybee a man to death."

Now was the bright time to shut up. Instead I said, "You can't have it both ways."

"I been hearing that since I was five. Why not this time?"

"Either we messed up by going in early on a good case,

or we brought you an uncrackable case and what we did didn't matter. Which is it?''

He turned back to Jon. "Which does Frees think I got?''

Jon stared out the window. "He thinks you can't get him. He as much as said so when we left: 'Talk all you want, but it don't mean a thing. I don't even need a lawyer till you say something with teeth in it.' ''

"Don't make fun of the way a fella talks,'' Farrell said mildly.

"I wasn't making fun. I thought you'd want to hear it word for word.''

"Right. Now listen up.'' He was back to me. "You without any badge at all except that mail-order cop kind. I can so have it both ways, 'cause I've got two targets for my mad. I'm mad at you two for breaking procedure when you should have known better and at Frees for thinking he can get away with this. I'm one hell of a lot madder at Frees, 'cause the chances are he's right.''

Frees was, and he knew it. After fifteen minutes of trying good-cop, bad-cop, leaning on him, dropping names and the usual, we'd crumpled up and driven off. He didn't even bother watching us from the window. He'd been shaken up by the pain of Colfax's death, but he wasn't worried about his own future.

I looked up at Farrell. "Can I ask you something?''

"Fire away. Might not answer. And I'll just ask you more questions, y'know.''

"I know. That's fine. Do you think Brian Frees is bright enough to think this up by himself?''

Farrell stared bleakly at me. "Brian Frees,'' he said slowly, "is not bright enough to get a license to pound sand. That's one thing bothers me. The other is that he isn't cruel enough to set anybody up for a slow death. And from what you tell me, he set up two nearly perfect murders. 'Course, I don't think anybody would have counted on Colfax's light sentence and easy time; that was pretty wild even for the courts these days. But Frees, doing that kind of planning?'' He snorted. "Brian Frees can't keep his wallet tight, let alone his mouth or his thoughts. He's got help. And I'd love to know who."

Jon said quietly, "Ask Emil Firebourne."

"Now you're jokin'."

"No, I'm not. He was the last client Roy Cartley had. That was what led us here."

Farrell looked skeptical. "You don't call a stranger so you'll have to kill him."

"Agreed. But why did Firebourne call him?"

Farrell opened his mouth, shut it. "You got me. Got me good." He scratched his head. "I may do some informal talking to Firebourne. You know what else?"

Jon nodded tiredly. I said, "What?" Straight man to the end.

Farrell put extra weight on each word. "You stay away from Firebourne till I've talked to him. Till I say go ahead. That goes double for Ada, his wife; she's been antsy lately, and there's no telling what she'd say. Stay away from both of them, till I say so."

I opened my mouth. Jon said, "We will."

I turned to look at him as Farrell said easily, "Well, that's settled. You two keep in touch if you come back to town." Jon nodded. After a second, I did too.

Outside I said, "I want to talk to Firebourne."

Jon said wearily, "If you try it now, that's all it'll be — just talk. If Farrell goes, he'll have his badge on, and he'll be able to push harder than you can."

"You trust him to do a good job?"

Jon snorted without humor. "You think we did a good job without badges when we talked to Frees? I'm not a cop down here. You never were a cop." He said to the ground, "I never shoulda come."

I shut up. Even so, I thought Farrell was more anxious than he needed to be about keeping us away from Ada and Emil Firebourne.

I talked Jon into one more trip. The banks were open late on Thursday nights for farmers. But when money is tight, people avoid banks if they can. It was farmers' banking hours, and the lobby was empty. The bank was doing its best not to notice.

First National was a glass-wall and red-brick affair with metal-frame doors and paneled walnut tables. On the wall was a picture of the old bank: marble counters and oak furnishings in a building so dark the hanging lights were halfway down to the floor. The old bank looked solider.

We knocked on the president's door, which was open. The man who looked up had silver-gray hair, steel-rimmed glasses and a firm jaw even when he smiled. "What can I do for you?"

"Are you busy?"

"Not that busy." He stood and shook hands. You don't get a grip like that from counting money. "Robert Huffman."

"I'm Nathan Phillips, and this is Jon Pederson. We're from Minneapolis." Jon showed his badge, which saved me the embarrassment of not having one.

Huffman raised an eyebrow. "If this is about me, I'd love to speak to a lawyer."

"Nothing about you." Jon smiled, but it was his business smile, the one that preceded tough questions. "Mr. Huffman, you may refuse to answer anything we ask you —"

"And we would understand if you did," I put in. "Our questions concern your customers, not your bank or your personal affairs."

"Mmmm." Huffman looked at me over his glasses. His eyes were clear, his face untroubled. If he had worries, he hid them well. "This is a small bank. We may turn down loans and we may force payment from people, just like the big banks do, but all business here is personal business." He waved an arm at the lobby. "We're no Swiss bank, but I figure those people have a right to privacy."

Jon looked annoyedly at me. I ignored him. "If that's really true, I want to open an account."

Huffman chuckled, then shrugged. "Ask," he said cheerfully. "If I feel I can answer, I'll be glad to. First, suppose you tell me what this is about."

And to my immense surprise, Jon told him. Laid it all out, with some detail, and finished, "We don't know why Nate's partner was killed, and we don't have enough evidence" — he didn't look at me — "to sound out our only lead. We're betting Roy was murdered for money: you don't kill total strangers for much else." Jon glanced casually out the window, even though it was too dark already for him to see much. "Since a stolen Rembrandt or a bank job would've made a lot of news in this town, and since no one has told us about either of those, we thought it might be investment money." He spread his hands. "So here we are."

"Money or debt?" Huffman wasn't smiling now. "There's a big difference — or there used to be."

"Why 'used to be?' " I looked casually at his desk. A roll of adding-machine tape stretched across it, five or six digits to a column.

He followed my glance. "Just balancing figures. But that's my point, Mr. Phillips." He stressed the name, probably to show he remembered it. "You can't tell, unless I tell you, whether that column is plus or minus. All the same, it's a lot of money — if it is money — and you're impressed." His smile was back. "Looks like a hell of a lot, doesn't it? That's the way business is in this town just now — a few people have big shops, or big cars, or big houses, but what most folks don't know is that those are just big debts."

He sighed. "Couple years ago a friend of my boy's" — he gestured to a picture of a grinning young man in a baseball uniform — "got married. That boy had everything for his wife: a classic Cadillac convertible, brand-new furniture, silver, china, Persian carpets. Everybody was impressed — except for young Rob and me. We fought like hell to get him out of all those deals, but it was no use. Eventually — pretty quickly, to tell the truth — he fell behind in his payments, and the dealers took their goods back. He lost the money and the goods. Are you getting my drift?''

Jon nodded, and I stared out the window at Belle View. On the side street some of the stores had false fronts, the kind people used to tack on to one-and-a-half-story buildings to make them look square-fronted and impressive. Suddenly, the whole town looked like a movie set, all propped walls and temporary roofs, waiting for a crew to dismantle it piece by piece.

I said softly, "How big a debt would it take to bring most of the town down?''

He looked at me sharply. "Couldn't be done. Oh, you could bring a couple banks down easily — though I don't think you could get mine," he added, sitting even taller. "But a few million in bad debts would force some of these loan companies and banks to call in the rest of their paper — which generates more bad debts." He looked from Jon to me uneasily.

"Now, don't start thinking about those Ohio banks that had runs. We're not talking about anything that drastic. This would simply be a matter of having to get a bigger bank to come in and take over. Most of the time people hardly notice that," he added with just a touch of bitterness. "Sign on the door changes, and nobody cares."

Jon said heavily, "Mr. Huffman, what we'd really like if you could do it is for you to give us a list of investors who might be in trouble for one reason or another. One of them may have found an outside source of money. One he'd be pretty anxious to hide."

He smiled, not happily. "Check the papers. Most of us are in trouble just now." I was intrigued by that "us."
"This town is mostly a marketplace for farmers; if they go, it goes. And they're going. About the only thing I'd guess would survive" — he jerked his head toward the office window — "is the B and V elevator. A man named Danny

Lowenbach took it over from the Co-op and made it a paying proposition. My guess is that it would be able to hang tough until the agri-businesses took over everyone's property." He shook his head. "Except that I want to keep in business, I hope I never see that. My father approved the mortgages on most of these farms."

Jon wasn't interested. I was frankly confused. I said, "Mr. Huffman, I haven't done that much financial investigating." His smile got broader. "Okay, I've hardly done any. Does anyone check financial records on people in this town?"

"The IRS. Some of the partnerships, like the grain elevator and the *News-Messenger*, hire a CPA to review the books. Looking for dirty work at the crossroads?" He was clearly intrigued.

"Beats me. You say, 'review the books.' I thought most folks used computers now."

"That's true, but people still keep printouts. And I doubt there's a CPA that doesn't know how to use spreadsheets." I must have looked puzzled, he added, "Spreadsheets — those programs that store, add, subtract, whatever, columns and tables of figures. If you're looking for computer piracy, forget it." But he looked thoughtful.

I barely needed to say it. "It's pretty easy to change numbers in those programs, or to make two copies of the same file on a computer, isn't it? An investor could keep two sets of books, maybe show debts as profits or the other way around —" I wished I knew more about finance and fraud. "Anyway, he could fool partners, maybe even a CPA, couldn't he?" I finished lamely.

He didn't laugh at me, and he didn't say anything. Jon said tiredly, "You know the answer to that, Nate. You're really asking if anyone around here would know how."

"Guess I am."

Huffman, who had watched us, chuckled. "Glad to know it can be done. But we're not that modern." Still, his gaze flickered to the computer on his desk, and I could tell

I'd given him something to worry about besides other people's bankruptcies.

We shook hands and left, no better off than we were before. On the way out, Jon cashed a check for enough to cover a bus ride — nothing like a helpful bank president when you need ready cash.

Jon bought a sandwich, and I dropped him off at the trailways stop. It was the Harvest Hotel, a drab brick building from the thirties; the bus pulled up to the side and a kid ran into the faded lobby to yell, "Twin Cities bus."

We shook hands. It felt silly when we'd see each other in a day or two. "Work day tomorrow?"

Jon grunted, "Sure. What about you?"

"In a manner of speaking. Take it easy." He got on and I went back inside to book a room.

The night clerk was on, a middle-aged woman with a permanent and a two-foot stack of magazines. I said, "Where's a good place to go in this town?"

"My kids have asked me that for years. Know what I tell them? 'Minneapolis.' " But she smiled. "Country Corner is the pizza place. Isn't any movie theater, but *Gone With the Wind* is on TV tonight."

I thanked her. "You're welcome. You in town on business?"

I said yes. That night I ate a Canadian bacon pizza (something I'd never heard of and wouldn't recommend), drank a couple of beers (something I don't ever recommend alone), and fell asleep way too late, after Scarlett had married Rhett. I'd seen it five times before. Sometimes it's nice to know how things are going to turn out.

Chapter Nine

I avoided even tea at breakfast. I was slow and fuzzy-headed, but somehow I didn't expect trouble in downtown Belle View on a weekday morning. I did have a glass of milk and an antacid; for the next hour or two, I'd be living on caffeine.

Farrell didn't want me talking to Emil Firebourne, and Jon thought that Farrell was right. But Jon didn't know small towns, and Farrell didn't know how well I knew them; if you look carefully enough, in every little town you'll find a retiree that knows people's lives as fully as they do themselves. Gossip, in small towns, takes the place of local radio stations; with some sharp questions and a little luck, I could find out about Firebourne without getting on the sherriff's nerves. I might even try to find out about Sheriff Josh Farrell.

There's a special peaceful secretiveness to early morning on a small-town Main Street. You see a young mother strolling a baby, maybe an old farmer and his wife with the pickup in town, running errands, but that's about it. The real life is behind the store windows, has been for hours. Owners are inventorying, book balancing, ordering the same amounts they did last year, trying to guess what's new and will sell — wafer-thin calculators, or Cabbage Patch Kid copies, or fake zebra-skin blouses. Maybe this time of year things were a little busier inside; Christmas decorations come out at Thanksgiving, but Christmas orders go in even earlier. Nine-tenths of everyone's life is invisible; in small towns there are few enough people to make one notice that.

By full daylight I could read the sign, a black frame with white letters following underneath the lights: Crystal Café. The booths had poles with coat hooks, and the tables had wood shelves with silvered railings for the sugar, the salt and pepper and the napkin holder. The tables were jet black, and they shone.

I ambled to a table opposite a booth with an elderly man in it and sat back quietly, facing the back. If you want to talk to strangers, sit close and don't sit where you can stare out. If that doesn't work, look bored.

A woman with a lapel pin that said "Cora" gave me tea and a cinnamon doughnut, and my neighbor said quietly, "Those are the freshest."

I turned and smiled at him. He nodded gently but repeatedly over a half-full cup, his silver hair fine enough to sway even with the small motion. His body was practically hidden by a dark sports coat that had been new during the Vietnam War. Back then he had worked in it; probably it had been tight on him.

"That's good to know. They made around here?"

"Across the street."

I obediently turned to look at Kruger's Bakery, a cursive neon sign in a store window full of wrapping-paper signs for sales. There was nobody in sight. "Is Mr. Kruger in?"

"Mr. Kruger's never in. He used to come in regular, about five every morning, and walk a batch of cinnamon doughnuts over here fresh at six forty-five. One morning he did bills first and shot himself. None of us even knew there was a gun in his desk." He acted as though they should have. "Noreen took over, and for a while we were scared she'd forget the doughnuts. She missed one week, but she hasn't since. If you get here at seven, when the door opens for business — you gotta knock before that — they're still hot." He stopped nodding and turned my way. "You from out of town?" he said, deadpan.

"From the Twin Cities. Nathan Phillips." I stood up.

"Homer Cortland." He extended his hand again. His grip was strong for a moment, then trembly. "What you do for a living?"

"I'm a private investigator."

"That sounds interesting." But he was being polite, and I warmed to him.

"It isn't very. Mostly I read old phonebooks, look for lost dogs, and hunt through people's check stubs, motel bills, and restaurant tabs. Sometimes I get shot at. That used to be fun. Now I love the dull parts."

One side of his mouth quirked up. Maybe he'd had a stroke. He seemed to smile down at me even while he was little and hunched. "The dull parts get pleasanter and pleasanter as you get older." He sighed. "Luckily, they also get longer and longer."

I agreed, even though I felt forced to look for the exciting parts just now. I thought about Jon's apparent lack of finesse in Huffman's office and how well it had worked. Why not? "I'm investigating the death of a friend."

He raised an eyebrow. It wouldn't stay up long, so he just squinted. "Why?"

Why? "Uh, because I think he was murdered."

"I figured that. Why not leave it to the police?"

That threw me. There were some things I wasn't ready to say. "I talked to a cop in Minneapolis, and I talked to your sheriff here, and I don't think they're going to investigate it." Not strictly true: Jon was giving up a bad job, and I didn't trust Farrell's competence, or his motives.

"Don't you think they know best?" He seemed awfully earnest. "Son, I don't know anything about what you're looking into, but I have seen — I do know that lots of times there's a sudden death, even a violent one, and there's nothing you can do. It's nobody's fault. Things like that, you're better not thinking of them."

I said stubbornly, "Even if somebody gets away?"

He dropped his eyes. "I guess you think catching some-one'll make it better. You'll learn. Well." He shook his head. "So why does it bring you to breakfast here?"

Maybe I'd better back off the open approach. "Just having my coffee. I'm on a break, and I thought I'd get to know the town." It sounded lame even to me. "To be honest."

He grinned. "To be honest, I come here to get to know the town, too. I've been on a break myself since seventy-four — the year, that is. Care to join me?"

I nodded. I'd meant to invite him, but he was faster than I was, and smoother, and possibly a lot smarter.

He tilted his head up. "Gertie! Tom! Company."

An immense woman in a blue dress shifted her massive neck to look at us, then sighed and struggled to her feet. Her companion, a man who in any other company would look fat, glared at us and followed her meekly.

Homer whispered quickly, "She's called Boopsie — not to her face. Hell of a square-dance caller, but lately she shouts so that it scares folks." I kept a straight face, and wondered if that disappointed him.

I let Boopsie — Gertie — slide in. Tom slipped in beside Homer, so I pulled a chair over.

"All right, Gertie?" He turned back to me. "Gertie had some trouble with the law."

"That's too bad," I said politely. "Traffic ticket?" I sipped my tea."

Homer shook his head. "Assault." Tom pounded my back harder than Homer could have. At least he got his reaction. He went on, "It's the real truth. She conked

Gladys Frye on the head with a frozen roast in the middle of Burke's IGA.''

"Last roast on sale." Gertie's voice was deeper than Homer's. I hadn't expected a woman who wasn't chain-smoking to sound that deep. "I saw it first."

" 'Course you did, Gertie." Tom nodded hastily. He seemed afraid of her.

Cora refilled cups for the others while I worked on mine.

Homer held his cup out. "No cream, Cora, you know that. Folks, this is Nathan Phillips, private eye. He's on break just now" — he caught my eye — "to be honest." I flinched. He went on: "But I'll bet he's here in town to dig up some old crimes." If he'd meant to stir their curiosity or warn them, he'd done it without giving away any of my business.

Gertie thumped the table. "I wasn't trying to kill Gladys. Even though she deserved it." She added darkly, "I didn't run down the Breitman kid's bicycle, either."

"Nobody thinks you did, Gertie." Tom looked at us each anxiously; from the expression on Homer's face, it had probably been true a minute ago.

I smiled, politely I hoped. "Actually, I'm working on something pretty specific." Card-laying time again. "A few years ago someone from Belle View tried to hire my partner for confidential business. Someone else — also from Belle View, I think — set my partner up to be murdered." Their eyes widened at that, and I felt cheap. Now Roy was good gossip. "I'm here trying to find out who arranged the murder and why."

Homer stirred his coffee slowly, staring at the swirls of light. "I didn't expect you to tell all this. I figured you'd make up a story for us." He glanced sideways at Gertie, and I wondered what was crossing his mind.

"Believe me, I wish I was making it up."

I went on, hoping I wouldn't sound foolish. "Stan Colfax — the kid that died the other day — killed my partner, not so much by accident as it looked."

"There." Gertie tapped her cup against the saucer. "What'd I tell you?"

Tom shifted on the seat. "Of course you did, Gertie. I'm sure you did. But I can't remember what you told me."

Her eyes snapped fire as they narrowed. Even twenty years ago, she'd have been a seriously passionate woman; maybe, to Tom, she still was. "I told you that Colfax boy never got drunk and drove before. I always thought something was strange there."

"If you recall," Homer said mildly, "You also said it was a first offense and that Stanley Colfax wouldn't hurt a fly." He nodded to me. "Just keeping the facts straight."

Gertie sputtered, but he took no notice. Probably five times a week they fought, and the rest of the week they looked forward to it.

"That's all I know, folks. My problem is that I don't know your town. I grew up in Walnut Grove; I know small towns have their scandals and secrets the same as big cities." I yawned. " 'Scuse me. Who here has a secret worth killing for?"

As I said it I knew how badly I'd phrased it. Tom looked terrified, and even Gertie shrank against the wall. Homer wrapped his loose coat tightly around his body, as though a chilly wind had blown through the café. "Nobody," he said faintly. "Nobody."

"Right. So nothing's worth killing for. Do you know someone who might think something was?"

That woke them back up. It was a nice question; you could answer it without accusing anyone, and it involved personal abuse.

"There's folks fool around here — married folks," Tom said eagerly. "Maybe they don't want —"

"Murder's a bigger crime." Homer tapped his spoon on the table, cheering up even more when it seemed to annoy Gertie. "You don't do something big to hide something little."

"Good point. But what's big?" I sounded too patient,

too patronizing, like I was teaching night school to slow adults. I sipped more tea, hoping the caffeine would kick in. I'd seen other people in cafés like this, in small towns and tight neighborhoods; if you were polite and friendly they'd tell you more than they would under three hours of grilling by expert interrogators. And they could see inside your skull when you were afraid about money, or angry, or worse.

Gertie said flatly, "You murder to hide murder."

"How right you are." I couldn't say more than that, but it was enough. "Any unexplained deaths around here?"

"No." They said it in unison, rapidly but regretfully.

"Right. Any big debts? Not farm debts," I added hastily, and they shut their mouths. "Any secret debts — gambling, or embezzling, or wildcat investments?"

"We lost a loan company to an embezzler named Cory." Homer stroked his half-shaven chin thoughtfully. "Was that two years back?"

"Three." We looked at Tom. "Three in January. His boy Pat was my paper boy. The morning his Dad confessed, Pat wobbled down the street on that cheap Schwinn and heaved a paper through the bottom storm on my front door. Only time he ever missed."

"No luck there, then. Any other business losses lately?" I looked from face to face.

Homer slumped forward tiredly. "Who knows?" He waved a hand. "You find out when they don't open one morning. You come by at ten and it's still locked. At eleven you tap your keys on the glass and go around to the back when nobody comes. If you're lucky, the door's open and you'll be the one finds the body and calls the cops."

He sighed. "Everyone's surprised till the story's made the rounds once; then they all say they knew it was coming."

Tom said softly, "Still bothers you, doesn't it?"

"Lots of things bother me. Finding Kruger, sure." He turned to me. "Something you wouldn't know, Nate: Two years after I retired, my old business, Cortland Jeweler — Werner's then; Corner Jeweler now — went belly up. Johnny Werner came down to my house on June first and cried like a little kid, and him forty-two. Trouble was, I couldn't do a thing. He owed the bank, and my money was tied up. Happens all the time, if you ain't some country that's borrowed two million. Then you get all the extensions you need." He shrugged. "I wasn't hurt, but the store I'd built from nothing was broke up and sold. The same thing's happened loads of times since."

"It happens too often." I frowned, not really paying attention. This wasn't helping much. "Tell me, is there anyone else who knows as much about this town as you people do?"

"Not many." Homer smiled, at least. "I've lived here since before the war. Hell, I've lived here since before the Depression. There's not many can say that." He looked at Gertie and Tom; Tom nodded eagerly, Gertie grudgingly.

Gertie leaned forward and stuck a pudgy index finger against the formica. "What about Arlis Schmidt?"

"True." Homer sat back, and all three of them looked significantly at each other.

"Alice Schmidt?" I said politely. Missing a well-known name always gets a correction and an explanation.

Surprisingly, it was Tom who took the bait. "Arlis. A-R-L-I-S." He watched me write it down. "She used to come here every morning and sit till lunch. By noon she could tell you 'bout everyone in town, and she never said half what she knew." His voice had the awe the gifted amateur has for the professional.

"How could I see her?" They told me where she lived. They seemed eager to send me there. "Can I pay for your coffee, folks? I'm on an expense account." Which wasn't true, but might establish goodwill. "Well, thanks for talking. I'm off to see Arlis."

Tom looked to be struggling with himself, but Gertie

spoke first. "Don't be disappointed if you hear more about Jesus than about the rest of us." She snickered.

"She's got religion now?"

"She always had it." I turned to look at Homer. "Just not in bulk. She has enough to give away now." He nodded to me. "Nice talking with you, Nathan."

I thanked them and left. I suspected that was what they wanted, and the only reason they'd sent me to see Arlis Schmidt. Before I was out the door they were at it a mile a minute, guessing about my business and speculating about who I'd investigate. I dawdled by the coat rack long enough to hear "Lowenbach," Cavenaugh," First National," and "Firebourne."

Homer glanced my way and signaled semi-furtively to the others. They shut up and stared. I waved and left, wild to know how much else I might have learned.

Chapter Ten

By noon it would be over seventy — a gorgeous Indian Summer day. I thought of going back for my car, then smu.ged. Arlis Schmidt lived on the edge of town, such as town was. That made it a ten-minute walk. I passed the fire station, the post office, the crossing grade where the railroad tracks used to be. I wasn't in any hurry.

The curb stopped before the railroad bed, but the houses on the other side weren't new. Most of them were the Midwestern version of salt boxes: short front roofs, back roofs almost down to the first floor. Only the nearest house on the left was a standard, square frame house with white siding.

The garden was by the railroad grade. The folks at the café had said I'd know Arlis Schmidt's yard anywhere, and they weren't kidding. It was twenty feet wide and fifty feet deep, every inch of it packed. There were flat limestone steps criss-crossed with sunken concrete blocks. A steel Ferris wheel with pots hanging in the place of gondolas stood next to a four-foot church with red window sills, cellophane stained-glass windows and a black spire two feet high.

The church walls were concrete, with stones, pieces of china and broken glass pressed in. So were the sides of the windmill, the skyscraper, the barn and the one-room schoolhouse. In West Bend, Iowa, there's a fancier place than this, The Grotto of the Redemption, a maze of rock-and-cement niches and walls and shrines. My friend Dave, who took me there, calls it Our Lady of the Lawn Ornaments. This garden was like that.

Of course, West Bend doesn't have an eighty-year-old woman in a white sweater and a print dress who tends the plants. I walked to the link fence bordering the garden and opened the gate. "Mrs. Schmidt?"

She turned quickly, with barely a trace of wobble. "Goodness. You startled me." She peered over her glasses, then through the top lenses, finally through the reading part. "Do I know you, young man?"

"I don't think so, ma'am." I was getting up to where I enjoyed being called "young man."

She threaded her way expertly between the last zinnias and the border of late marigolds. Behind her the first bagged rose bushes stood like ghosts. Any money she used white bags so they wouldn't contrast with the snow later. "Are you a Schwickerson?" She touched my shoulder delicately, then pulled back. "I knew a Schwickerson had rounded shoulders like that."

"No, ma'am. That's from a desk job. I'm —"

"A Vahlstedt? You don't have the blonde hair, but there was Peggy Vahlstedt; she had brown hair. Not since 'fifty-nine or 'sixty though, poor thing . . . you a Rolvaag, maybe?"

I shook my head. "I'm not from around here. My name's Nathan Phillips." I took off my hat. I'd worn it on purpose to take off.

"Pleased to meet you. Did you come to see me, or to look at the garden?" She cocked her head to one side, partly like a bird and partly like a teenage flirt.

"I came to see you, of course, but I'm very impressed with the garden." "Impressed" was a nice, neutral word. "I was told to take a good look at it."

She nodded. "There's lots of people come just to see the garden." She spread her hands, and I noticed how clean her cotton gloves were. "The kiddygarten classes come here every spring. I bake cookies for two days first. You have to imagine it in May."

I could. Ignoring the little buildings, which kids would love, it would be delightful. "Any tulips?"

"Tulips, daffodils, hyacinths — crocuses first, of course. Sometimes they come right up through the last of the snow. Oh, and snowdrops." She ticked them off. "And the second wave hits with the first of the lilacs."

I hadn't noticed the bushes beyond the garden. "What about these vines?"

"On the fence? The ones next to the railroad are sweet peas. I should pull them up," she confessed. "They're just weeds. But they're so pretty, and the Lord sent them."

"Right. Uh, I also came to ask you some questions —"

"You're that private detective in town, aren't you?"

I stared at the rocking pots in the Ferris wheel before answering. "That was fast. Am I in the paper?"

"The *News-Messenger*?" She sniffed. "Maybe in a week or so. Folks still drop by or call me, and they tell me lots of things. Sometimes things they shouldn't. I used to be such a wicked gossip." Again she sounded faintly flirtatious.

"Mrs. Schmidt, I'd like to talk to you for a few minutes, if it wouldn't be too much bother."

"No bother at all." She stepped back, a shy girl being asked to dance.

"I'm afraid I'm going to make you remember your wicked ways, if I can."

"Why, Mr. Phillips!" She opened the gate and motioned me to follow her to the front door. I was company.

On the front lawn she paused and glared at the nearly immaculate lawn under a silver maple. I stared, but saw nothing. "Something bothering you?" The tree itself, yellow and orange this time of year, was perfect.

"Another one." Finally I saw it: a single leaf, resting in the shadow of the tree. "And I swear, I just raked before you came."

"I believe it. This is the best-kept lawn I've ever seen."

That got a wide smile. She either had good teeth or great dentures.

Her parlor was about what you'd expect on a sitcom about the Midwest. That threw me; everyone else I knew had furniture from catalogues, not from farm auctions. There was a genuine horsehair sofa, and an overstuffed chair with a faded blue slipcover and pleated skirt. The mahogany coffee table had curved legs with oak leaves and acorns at the top. All the furniture was dust free, and all the wood shone and smelled faintly of lemon. It was like a museum. On the wall I saw an old tintype of a woman with her hair in a bun; at a guess it was Arlis's grandmother.

I sat down carefully, but the sofa didn't wobble. The seat, particularly, was hard. Arlis heard me shifting and called, "Make yourself comfy. I'm just putting the kettle on." She added, "Why don't you find yourself something to read?"

Why not? To start with, the glass-fronted bookcase in the corner had *Pilgrim's Progress, Moby Dick, Little Women, Robinson Crusoe* and the other staples of antique bookshelves. Usually you can learn about people from what they read; I was learning about somebody who couldn't possibly still live here.

The only other reading material was on the coffee-table: *National Geographic*, featuring the Sierra Nevada, and a set of pamphlets printed in two colors on cheap paper. I

leafed through them: WORKING WIVES — WORTH THE SOR-
ROW? THE PAPACY AND ASSASSINATION. THE COMMON
MARKET AND PROPHECY. The first two came from the
same Arkansas publisher.

I settled back with the third one. It's nice to think that
St. John the Divine was so on top of European economics
and socialism. It ended with an exhortation to prepare for
the world to come and a list of available pamphlets and
suggested donations.

Mrs. Schmidt came back in, scarf off and patting her
hair. "I hope you're comfortable. Oh, I see you've found
them. If you want, take that one with you; I'm done with
it."

"So am I. This room is amazing; are the pieces all
heirlooms?"

"Oh, yes — well, that lamp used to be a kerosene
lantern, but Ray Riley converted it for me. He's such a
clever boy." I wondered how old he was. "Yes, these
pieces were all my grandmother's, and my mother's after
that. I got them back from the rest of the family a few
years ago." She perched in the overstuffed chair trium-
phantly, and I realized, as I should have after seeing the
garden and lawn, how strong willed she was.

"It's pleasant to sit in a room that's so —" I waved an
arm.

She nodded, thank God. "It's all just so. Not a thing out
of place." Casually she moved my hat to the arm of the
sofa; I'd left it in the middle of the table. "And, you
know, that's just what I like about God's will. He looked
at it, and He saw that it was Good." She looked me
straight in the eye while I was trying to duck. "And you
can bet it was Tidy, too."

"Right, right. Mrs. Schmidt, I don't know what you've
heard about why I came here —"

"You don't?" She was actually surprised. "Oh, of
course you wouldn't know. You don't know who to talk
to, do you?"

"I'm learning." I had to; I wasn't allowed to talk to Firebourne.

That got a smile. She glanced at the pendulum clock on the bookshelf. "Well, this won't take long."

I'm pretty good at investigating. I learn who to question, I ask the right questions, and I keep my eyes open. And; by God, I knew inside of five minutes what an amateur I was. Arlis Schmidt knew about Roy. She knew about Jon, and about Colfax, and about the answers we'd gotten from Frees. And she suspected I was going out with someone, though how in the hell she guessed that was beyond me, and I thought she made more of the romance than there actually was. Maybe she read tea leaves.

She paused for breath and looked at the clock. "There. Four minutes."

"And an educational four minutes it was. Mrs. Schmidt, I'm wasting my time down here. Could I just hire you?"

She blushed as best an old woman can, but shook her head. "You mean well, but that's no thing to drag a woman into."

"Women have changed."

"No; talk has changed. It ain't nothing to drag *anyone* into. You say I'd do a better job than you." She cocked her head on one side, this time with no flirtation in the pose. "Will you listen to my advice, then?"

"I'd be a fool not to."

She sighed like a frustrated six-year-old. Lively old people aren't just old; they're the sum of their ages. "I don't mean rudeness, but we've all been fools, haven't we? But here's my advice: go back to Minneapolis and don't look for revenge. Vengeance is mine, saith the Lord."

I sat back. "That's moral advice —"

"It's also practical."

"— but I don't want revenge. I want justice."

She looked at me with pity. "You do, don't you? And you don't know what that means yet. Mr. Phillips, we talk careless. We say justice is a good thing, like freedom or sunshine. It's a terrible thing, a horrible thing. Men and women getting exactly what they deserve. Reckless people get pain, cruel people get torment, heartless people spend years weeping." She glanced at the Bible on the bookshelf. "I'm not saying they wait for Hell, either. I'd rather have mercy, and that's why I'll give it. You better learn to want the same."

I shifted uncomfortably, maybe because none of this was what I needed. "I'll certainly think about it, ma'am." I coughed. "I guess since you no longer spend much time downtown you don't know your neighbors the way you used to."

She looked up from straightening the already-straight table. "I know that Pat Cavanaugh went to the bank first of the month and had a long talk with Lyle Peterman about extending credit. I know that Riley Rambler, Kevin Riley's place, used to keep two sets of books. I know that two of those gossips downtown plan to move in together, and think nobody knows. I know that Ada Firebourne told Emil that he's got to get his cash back out of the granary, the Firestone building, and the loan to the *News-Messenger*, or she's going back to her sister's. And I know enough not to trust that Danny Lowenbach."

Bingo. Emil Firebourne had two bad investments out of three, and trouble at home. Whatever the people at the café had thought they were doing when they sent me here, they'd done me a favor.

"Guess I wasn't too tactful, Mrs. Schmidt. You do stay informed."

She looked troubled. "Actually, I try not to, these days. And I also try not to say much." She bit her lip like a young girl. "You tricked me."

"I'm afraid I was trying to. I need to know as much as I can about" — I hesitated — "people here."

She settled back in the overstuffed chair. "I can see you have a way with people. I might as well tell you what you need to know."

"I don't have half the way you do." I meant it. "Do people in Belle View run to business gambles?"

"Not now. You should have been here ten years ago." She wasn't focused on the room, but her eyes were clean and sharp, and she was frowning. "We used to call them the Young Tigers."

"Who?"

"Why, the sharp-suited young men that came out here to make everybody rich." She gave the only nasty smile I ever saw on her, then or later. "Land prices were high. Farmers could borrow as much as they wanted. My, but everyone was nice to us then. You could wear overalls into a bank — not that I did, of course; I mean farmers — and the presidents and vice-presidents would shoot out to shake hands. Everybody's mail was full of pamphlets about money markets and securities and condos they could invest in if they wanted to or they were crazy. And all these young men came out in wide ties and shiny shoes, saying how they'd make retirement easy."

"Where are they now?"

"Where the money is. Wherever it went." She shook her head. "The business computer company folded. The farm machinery clearing house broke up the same month White Motor's plant started laying off. All the other things — land schemes, shopping malls, health clubs — never built anything beyond a nice front office with desks for the Tigers and one local."

"They're all gone?" I didn't see where this was leading.

"All but that Danny Lowenbach. Land prices went down, credit disappeared, and they all rolled up their businesses and left. Gone south, I think; that's where everyone says the money is. And they left a lot of bad debts and some worried people behind them."

"Nice guys."

She started. "Oh, they weren't all bad. I ought to be fair to That Danny —" She made it sound as though "that" was his first name. "He stayed on and made his business work. It nearly drove him under, but he's been under so many times, I suppose it didn't frighten him the way it does the rest of us.''

This was my meat. "Bad manager, was he?"

"My heavens, no. But he always invested in such wild schemes — the health club, and a thoroughbred racing farm out here, and an industrial park to attract a brewery —'' She laughed and shook her head. "They all sound crazy now, but my, how people believed him when he talked. He was a charmer.'' She tilted her head slyly. "Like you, Mr. Phillips.''

"Uh, thanks. I think. How did he stay solvent?''

"He didn't, exactly. But he took out some loans and bought the B and V granary, with some partners from his other deals. It was good to see him invest in something solid. That was five, six years ago, and today that granary is the soundest business in town. Audited regularly, too.''

She swayed back and forth, forgetting she wasn't in her rocker, maybe. "I hear he takes his share with him when he travels, trying to start another get-rich-quick business. The granery's too solid for him.'' She laughed. "Only scheme any of the Tigers made money on, and he's not happy with it. Well, well.''

"What about the people who bought into it with him?''

"Oh, they're perfectly happy. Except for Niles Swenson, who's never happy. And Emil. He kept borrowing against the earnings, I guess. Bought the Firestone building, and made some loans —'' She shook her head. "Emil Firebourne could turn anything into a bad debt. Ada's afraid he's done it again.'' She saw me reach for my pencil and notebook — I hadn't gotten that out yet — and she back-pedaled. "Well, you know what they say about the Lord's treasures on earth.''

I knew, all right. I knew a woman back home who could speak about it for forty-five minutes. I looked at my watch, wishing I had just let her go on about Emil. "Look at the time! Mrs. Schmidt, thank you so much for talking.

Could I come back some time? You're wonderful to talk to."

"Why, how nicely you put that. I've been an old gossip, haven't I?"

I said sincerely, "You've given me one of the most valuable hours I've ever spent in a strange town."

She tilted her head away and to one side, smiling. "Oh, now. You shouldn't talk so."

"Can't help it." I grinned and put on my hat as I stepped out, trying not to flourish. Some days I'm hell with the women.

Chapter Eleven

I pulled my car out from around back. The hotel manager, a bored, skinny man in a tight collar, asked me if I always hid my car.

I looked hard at him. "I bet I'm not the first man ever hid his car when he came here."

He ran a finger around his neck. "No, but you're the first ever did it and slept alone."

"Maybe when I came here I didn't plan on sleeping alone."

He grinned sickly. "God knows, I never do."

Before leaving I reconnoitered with the phone book (stolen from the hotel room) and my list of names from Arlis Schmidt: Pat Cavanaugh, Kevin Riley, Lyle Peterman, Danny Lowenbach, Niles Swenson, and of course Emil. Emil and Niles lived out of town; in a community this size it wasn't hard to locate the rest of them. Five miles later I knew where all the in-town principals lived and what their homes were like. Most of them lived at one end or the other of Ellwood or Oak streets, in the older houses in town. Danny Lowenbach had a flashier place, built recently on the edge of town, but even that was no mansion. Their cars were upscale Buicks, LTDs, one or two Lincolns, no Mercedes or Porsches. I bet there wasn't any place nearby to repair the foreign makes. So much for conspicuous consumption.

Work habits stay with you; at the edge of town I noted the mileage on my clipboard and pulled across the highway for gas.

On the brick facing wall you could see the unfaded spots where the Texaco sign used to hang. Now a new sign said simply, "Keller Gas."

The building itself was tan brick, exhaust-stained, but well kept up, with posters in the window for a high-school production of *Charley's Aunt*, a football schedule for the BV Bombers, and a flyer announcing a church spaghetti dinner.

The man who shuffled out to fill my tank was in a lot worse shape than the building. His belly came first by a good two or three inches. His coveralls, unzipped for his belly's comfort, said "Karl" in grease-smeared red over the shirt pocket. His once-red O'Shay Drain Tile cap was faded to a weak salmon by dirt. But his smile was clean, and he squinted through the windshield with piggy amiability. "If you're gonna park here, boy, you gotta get gas."

"If I gotta, I gotta. What say you check the oil and water?"

"If you got 'em, I'll check 'em." He rapped on the windshield. "Hood latch."

"Right." I unlocked the gas cap and stepped back as he grabbed the hose. He was humming somewhere just below a shout, occasionally singing scattered words about Lucille, farming and a broken heart.

He punctuated the concert with, "Water's okay," "Oil looks kind of pimpy and dirty, but she's okay," and "What's that dojigger on your speedometer cable?"

"What?"

"New thing. Little shiny box she is." He added admiringly, "Looks real fine. I'd get one for my Ford if I knew what the hell it did."

"Stop the pump."

"You upset?"

"Just stop the pump." He did. "Now back away. Away from the car. Now."

He didn't like my voice, and I didn't blame him, but I waited until he was ten feet off to talk or move again. I got out slowly, not closing the door and wincing when the car rose on its shocks. No bumping. "Sorry if I was rude. Where's the speedometer cable?"

"Ya don't know? Right —" He stepped forward, stopping as I gestured him back. "Over there by the steering column. Know where that is? Big long thing, pokes through the dash. The cable's metal wrapped."

I saw it, and I saw the new box, too. It did look nice — a fine piece of work, from the short cable to my odometer to the small wires dropping down below the engine.

Also, it had nothing to do with the car as far as I could tell. Not for the first time, I wished I knew something about cars.

I pulled away from the hood. "Call the sheriff."

Karl wrinkled his brow. "You know best, but I'll tell you right now he don't know much more about cars than you do."

I nodded, then did a double take. "Tell him to bring a bomb expert or whatever's closest to one around here."

His eyes popped open at that, and his grin expanded. "You're a pretty exciting fella; anybody ever tell you that?" He winked. "Just you watch this." He raised his voice above the usual bellow. "Virge? Hey, VIRGE! We got a terrorist attack out here."

An angry fifty-year-old in a crew cut poked his head out the green front door. "What the hell is it? I pay you, not your damn mouth —" He stopped when he saw me.

"There's a bomb on my car. Better cut the pumps."

He looked me up and down. "Hell I will. You get that car away from the pumps."

"I'm not starting it."

"Push it, then."

I walked back to the driver's side, checked the odometer. It was about to turn another tenth. And what would that silver box turn when it did, and would I be around to check?

I turned back to Virge. "No way, Mister Keller. You want it done, you do it."

He stood directly under the sign, glaring at me. "Now how did you know my name?"

It was a tough line to pass up. "Just look under the hood, okay? You'll see why I want an expert."

"All right, dammit." He walked up, peered, then went back into the garage. "Lemme get a better look." He had something in his left hand, some long-handled tool he wasn't giving me a good look at. He scuttled around to the driver's side and stared at the apparatus and looked pained.

"God's sake, is that all?" he said, and about the time I realized he was holding a bolt-cutter he whipped it forward and snapped my odometer cable in half above the box.

When I reopened my eyes, he had cut the cable below the box as well, and was looking back at me with a satisfied grin. Karl was peering into the motor. "Oil's fine. Water's fine. Bomb checks out okay, but that cable's a teensy frayed."

I walked into the garage and dialed Farrell. Virge and Karl rolled my car away from the pumps. At the moment I wasn't all that concerned about their safety.

I came back, calmer, with a can of Coke. Virge was back in the garage, swearing at a clutch plate. Karl was sitting on the pump island, watching my car. "Don't you worry about that cable. Ol' Virge, he's broke hundreds of those for people; he knows just what to do. Bet he's got a good used one he'll put in just like new. And it won't cost much more than twice what it would in a regular place —"

Virgil interrupted him with some timely advice on what to do with those lonely hours.

I sipped the Coke. "I'll take it to Minneapolis, thanks. I have a regular garage. Why are you watching my car?"

Karl said solemnly. "You never can tell. She might blow any minute."

I could see Virgil's side of things.

Farrell came without sirens and with a scrawny little dark-haired man who had only two fingers on his right hand. "Explosives expert?" I said faintly.

"Dooley Willardsen." He shook hands. "You'd be surprised, the stuff I've handled, and the accidents I've had."

"I'm sure I would," I said sincerely. "Sheriff, I —"

He didn't move, just looked. I shut up. He was The Law West of the Pecos today. Even Jon would freeze at that look; Farrell wanted me out.

Only Karl was unaffected. "Yo, Josh. Brought the deputy, I see." He saluted the paunch. "Yo, Dep."

"Shut up. Back up." Karl did.

Farrell turned to Virgil. "Apologize to the man. Say you're sorry about his new cable."

Virgil nodded. I said, "Thanks," just as though he'd gotten it all out."

Farrell said, "Karl, go home and do some farming. It's more than time you were gone."

Karl tipped his hat, then froze in place. Farrell wasn't done with him.

"Now, would the three of you like to take this a little more seriously? There was a try at a murder this afternoon. Phillips" — he jerked his head at me — "I can see getting careless about such things, since a day he doesn't see a corpse seems to be pretty rare. But would you two clowns" — Virge opened his mouth, shut it — "care to tell me what makes messing with evidence so easy for you?''

Virgil blinked, shuffled, suddenly growled, ''I got no time for this crap,'' and shuffled back into the garage.

Karl watched him go. ''Nice going, Josh. I don't see ol' Virge with his tail between his legs that often.'' He waved to me and ambled off.

Farrell grinned at me. ''Know what we called Virge in high school? Course you don't. The Vicious Virgin. Wonder if that's what made him so mean. I have to laugh, seeing him work with Karl; Karl's the best-tempered man I know. Smiles all the time, no matter how rough life is, farming evenings and jobbing to make it days.'' He turned to me. ''And now —''

Farrell was good at fast, sharp questions. He wanted fast, short answers, and I felt less and less like a civilian as I gave them. No, I didn't have a list of suspects; no, I hadn't parked my car under a light or where I could see it from a window. Yes, I'd give it some thought the next time I came down. No, sir, I wasn't trying to make fun. Yes, sir, I respected the law. No, sir, I had never spent a night in jail. Yes.

''Yes, what?'' His face was red, and he was standing a foot from me.

I stood ramrod straight, eyes front, and bellowed into his face, ''Sir, yes, sir!''

His jaw dropped and the iron went out of him. Karl, munching a Snickers, leaned out of his car. ''You forget again, Josh?''

''Sorry, boy. I was a sergeant. That does things to you.''

''That's all right. Sir.''

''You ever in the Marines?''

''I, uh, had a high lottery number.''

''Good thing,'' he said without rancor. ''Hate to think

what you'd've looked like if I'd gotten hold of you . . . well. So you don't know when it happened, and you don't know why?''

"No." I hesitated. "You want to know how it looks to me?''

"Not much." He spat. "Let's have it."

"I think Frees murdered Colfax; you know that. He as much as admitted it, but we can't prove it. I started asking questions this morning; that must have got back to him. He's not working alone — but we can't prove that, either.''

Farrell looked me in the eye a long time. It took an effort not to look away.

Finally he said tightly, "So, Colfax was a murderer. I sure-God can't touch him now, thanks to you. And you think Frees hired one murder and did another, and I can't touch him on either one, thanks to you and your city-cop friend. And someone else tried to blow you to God, hell, or Missouri today, and all the help you offer is some guesses. You always make people this happy?''

"Not if I can help it." I stared back. "I'll be glad when this is over.''

"You will, huh? Funny. I'm betting none of us will be." He tossed the pad he carried but hadn't written on through the driver's window of his car. "I can't make you leave town, Nate, but I wouldn't let you room with anybody I liked. We're not gonna catch the fella who did this soon. Don't know how, for one thing. For another, it could be anyone that knew cars, and that category is kinda big.''

I nodded. "I was just leaving. I'm coming back later, though. I may take time off my job." I took a deep breath. "That's when I'll talk to Emil." He didn't react. "I'll call before I come. And I promise I'll park my car where I can watch it.''

"Thanks. Might help some.''

Someone in a pickup honked as he passed. Farrell waved. The gun rack in the rear window had a rifle and a pump shotgun in it. Before this morning, I might not even have noticed the guns.

"What is it, deer season?" Farrell shrugged. I tried again. "Pheasant? Maybe both?"

"They might just be blasting at bottles on a fence post." He stared after the truck. "Then again, some things you can always shoot." He caught my eye. "Ever heard of open season?"

After a moment I nodded. I'd only been making small talk, but for me there wasn't any casual conversation in Belle View.

Dooley Willardsen came back up, rubbing his hands on a pair of Virgil's coveralls. "Wanna take a peek?" He held out the box.

Farrell groaned. "Dooley, you were s'posed to disarm it, not disassemble it. What about fingerprints?"

Dooley looked hurt and said a line I've repeated many times since. "I ain't dumb. I got a few of mine on it, but I wiped 'em all of." He tossed the parts up and down. We flinched, and he laughed. "Nah, nah, the charge is by the curb. Sucker was set on your gas line, far enough back so it wouldn't heat up. But look at this."

It was an odometer, set at twenty-five. Two thin wires ran from it. "I don't see how he did this," Dooley said admiringly, "but my guess is that when it turned one hundred, it'd go up and take you with it."

Farrell stared down the road. "Hundred's a good figure. Gets you back to the Twin Cities, only part way back here if you turn straight around. Makes it harder to connect this place with anything."

"You make that sound like a good idea."

"Not half bad, for an amateur," he said frankly. "That scares me more than if you blew apart on Main Street."

Something bothered me. "Dooley, did that counter start at zero?"

He cackled. "Don't ever buy used cars, young fella. Those odometers, you can start them anywhere you want.

Coulda been started at twenty-five, just before you pulled in."

"Twenty." I added for the sheriff. "I've been driving around for a while, getting acquainted. It had to be done at the Harvest Hotel, last night or this morning."

Farrell shook his head. "It had to be done in the last twenty-five miles. That coulda been driving out to Frees's place, or around town before that. Hell, you could set it back before zero and let it turn over, couldn't you?" He looked hopefully at Dooley.

Dooley scratched his chin with his good hand, frowning. "That could get tricky, Chief. See, to zero out, that third nine would have to move to zero, and I'd hate like hell to set it so careful that it didn't jiggle and connect when it turned over in a moving car. I wouldn't do it, myself," he said virtuously, scratching his nose with his scarred right hand.

"That settles it." Farrell didn't smile. "Okay, Nathan. It had to be done in my county. If I find anybody, I'll need you to tell me whether you've seen 'em before, help me figure out how they know you. That okay?" I nodded. "Good. Do us all a favor and stay out of trouble for a day or two."

I nodded and got back in the car, thinking about what would have happened if I hadn't stopped in.

Farrell watched me get in, then said casually, "Nate?"

"Yessir."

"Knock off the sir; I said I'm sorry. Where would you have been seventy-five miles from now?"

"Let's see . . ." I pictured myself driving up to my apartment, letting myself in. Feed Marlowe, let him back out if he wants — that doesn't put mileage on anything but me. Shave again, pick up Annie for dinner . . .

I started to sweat. Three miles. Drive to the restaurant. It's a nice night; want to take the river road?

That's all right, Nate, 95 is shorter. The Dinky-dale Deli okay?

Sure. Wouldn't want to hurt our budgets. A quick view out over the river, sunset turning the east bank red and hiding the west in shadows. Oh, Nate, you were right. We should have taken the river road.

Click.

Then the bang, and Annie'd just have time to turn my way before the flames move up the gas line to the tank. More than half a tank of gas. I like to top it off.

I opened my eyes. "I would have been with a friend, sheriff. And thanks a lot for asking. You just completely shot my night."

He didn't nod, didn't smile, didn't even act like he'd heard. "I kinda hoped I would."

Chapter Twelve

"It's not that funny." I seemed to be saying that a lot lately. I glanced around at the other diners jammed into Tony's on a Friday night. I wondered if anyone was listening.

"Oh, I don't know." Annie grabbed the last slice, pepperoni and all. She smiled at Dave Komarek, who had just told her about the time, when Marlowe was a kitten, that I'd put him on my shoulder and he'd slipped inside my shirt and panicked. "How much of your shirt did you leave unbuttoned, anyway?"

"Two, maybe three buttons. Look, I was hot."

"Or thought you were."

Dave said solemnly, "Oh, no, Anne. It was sure hot that night. But Nate thought he was cool, I think." He stared at her with those solemn dark eyes that always look half heartbroken. She laughed again. Dave was getting on my nerves tonight.

We'd come to Tony's because Dave had called: "Nate, I sure want to take you and this new lady to dinner, but I'm broke again. Is pizza okay?" I couldn't talk him out of paying, even by telling him how much Annie made. All he'd say was, "Then I sure don't want her thinking you and your friends are all deadbeats." What that "all" was doing in there I couldn't imagine.

So Annie had met Anton Schmidt, who runs Tony's, and Dave Komarek, who runs like a deer from serious romance, and now it was getting toward time for a movie. I said so.

Dave didn't notice my tone, didn't mind. "You make sure he pays, Anne." He stared at her earnestly. "And for gas, and popcorn and all that stuff. Nate, he can be awful cheap." He tossed his nearly black straight hair back over his forehead, where it had fallen while he'd hunched over the pizza and, I might add, the pitcher of beer. I'd only had one glass.

"I'll get every penny I can out of him," Anne said solemnly. "Nate, maybe this isn't the time to bring it up, but I kept the receipts from our last date. Cough up."

I did, mostly beer. "That was your turn."

"That was also provençale cooking. You just took me for pizza and got a friend to pay."

"Not yet." I glared at Dave. He looked hurt, then paid. I tried to chip in one last time, but he wouldn't let me. Annie even left the tip; she and Dave gave me hell all the way to the car about that.

When we were on the road she all but purred. "I'm stuffed. That was just what I needed."

"I'm glad to hear that. Look, I'm sorry it wasn't someplace fancier, but —"

"Oh, no. In a way, that was special, too."

"Special how?"

"If we kept going to fancy places, we'd go broke. This is more normal."

I hadn't thought of it that way. "Sure. Welcome to my life. You find Dave normal?"

"He's really sweet. What were you saying about Tony's?"

"Nothing. Just that I like Anton, and it's a favorite place of Dave's. Why are you smiling like that?"

"You don't like my smile?"

I had this overpowering urge to tell her how and how much I liked her smile. "No, no; you look — fine. Terrific. Anyway —"

"You went to the john tonight."

"A God-given right of beer drinkers. Better than the alternative. So?"

"So Dave told me about the rent."

"What about —? Ah, no. Damn." A couple of months back, Dave had fallen behind in his rent. He never said why he was broke, and I never asked. I wondered at the time why he hadn't gone to Bernie and only realized later that he probably had, the first time. "Okay. That's why he insisted on paying tonight."

"Because it's the only way he can pay you back just now."

"He's got lots of time. Hell, we're not forty yet." I felt embarrassed, but a little pleased that he'd told Annie. So far as I knew, he hadn't told Bernie or Sherri or anyone else.

"Stop acting tough; it doesn't suit you. What are you slowing for?"

"I can't be right." I stuck my head out of the window. "I am. Yo, Bernie! Hey!" I pulled my head back in. "This evening is about to become exciting."

She went rigid. "Somebody from your work?"

"Heavens, no. Anne, there's someone I'd like you to meet."

I made the introductions as Bernie pulled even with the car. He was in reasonably new brown sweats; he hadn't been using them long enough either to get them dirty or to lose much weight. "How come you're not jogging, Nate? It's a great night." He had two strips of fluorescent tape on his chest in a V, partly to alert drivers, partly to look broader shouldered. "You really ought to try it. Makes you better, fitter, healthier."

"I'm such a slob compared to you, Bern. How long you been at it?"

"Five or ten minutes."

"No, I don't just mean tonight."

"Neither did I. Don't you think he ought to jog, Anne? His job never gets him enough exercise —"

Anne stiffened, but the No Shop Talk rule didn't apply to Bernie. I said easily, "I'll try it. I promise. Right now we're headed for a movie."

"We are? Which one?"

I told him.

"Terrible. The special effects stink. Excuse me." Anne dazedly hunched forward as he got in the back. It was all too much like taking your kid brother on a date with you.

"I can tell you have a candidate."

Bernie leaned forward, pounding the seat for emphasis. Whatever running had done, it hadn't tired him. " 'Sensational' — *Newsweek*. 'A must-see' — *Time*. 'Taut, thrilling, spell-binding' — Siskel and Ebert."

" 'I haven't seen it yet' — Bernie." I could see it coming. "You're not dressed for the movies."

"Aw, c'mon. It's not black tie. You don't mind my coming, do you?" he said to Anne. She shook her head politely. Bad move. "See? Loan me five dollars, Nate."

"How expensive is this show?"

"Well, some of that's for popcorn." He patted his stomach. "I've earned it."

"Right." I pulled away from the curb. "Mind, Annie?"

She blinked. "I feel like I've been in a fender-bender."

"No, you've been run down by a movie addict. Is it okay with you if we change movies?" To my immense relief she said yes. There was no tactful way to explain in front of Bernie that going to the movies with him was like seeing a double feature.

He leaned forward. "It's on Lake. You're gonna have to gun it to make the second show." He leaned back again. "Boy, is this great. I was gonna have to *run* home," he added earnestly. I caught Annie's eye, and the two of us tried very hard to look sympathetic.

Bernie was too nervous; we got to the Studio One with a few minutes to spare. Nothing happened when we parked or when we paid, unless you count Bernie's telling the ticket taker that he was my date. Annie, behind us, announced that it was disgusting and as a member of Moral Majority she wanted us to know. The ticket taker was unimpressed.

Inside we stood in line for popcorn, eyeballed the posters for coming attractions, basically waited. Bernie hopped from foot to foot. He's lousy at waiting. He scanned the crowd.

Suddenly he cried in ecstasy, "Look!" Annie looked; I knew better.

This time all he did was streak across the lobby to a knot of people, mixed in age, gathered under a Harrison Ford poster. Several of them were talking. I couldn't make out the words.

Annie and I followed just slowly enough that we barely caught Bernie's opening salvo, to a classically elegant blonde in her late twenties. She was everything Bernie's big loves never were, with short-cropped hair, modest earrings, light makeup, preternatural self-control. She didn't even flinch as Bernie said, too loudly, "Look, I know I shouldn't do this, but you're wonderful and I'm really excited. Could we please, please, please go out?"

She stared at him. I've seen that look before, mostly on boxers in the eighth round or on people who have just met Bernie.

"When would be convenient? Look, if you want me to go away, just say so."

By now Annie, trying to look uninvolved and still not miss anything, had caught up with him. The woman's eyebrows puckered, and she looked agonizedly to one side at the group that had just drifted silently away from her.

It hit me. Sweet God, Bernie's pestering a mute. I whipped out a pen and an envelope from my jacket pocket.

She barely looked at me as she scribbled. Bernie tried to see over her shoulder. "What are you doing? Speak to me. Look, I don't mean to be offensive. Usually. I don't always act like this."

She didn't look impressed. After seeing Bernie pop out of nowhere in sweats and declare his love to a total stranger in a crowd, who would be?

She folded the note in half and passed it to Bernie, who took ten seconds unfolding it. I looked over his shoulder:

"*Regrese alla casa de los monos, tonto. 555-3947.*"

Below that she had written, in parentheses, "*Cortesia del* Minnelang."

I would have pocketed the note. Bernie didn't have pockets. He simply waved the note over his head and called, "Excuse me. Does anyone in here speak Spanish?"

This time she flinched, even while trying to blend into the group she'd been in before. They all turned around, and a few people moved hesitantly toward Bernie, then sensibly back.

An elderly woman nearby, the kind Bernie always plays on the sympathies of, said, "Why, yes. Is it an emergency?" She obviously knew what was going on.

He handed her the note. "You tell me. It's from a woman —" He stopped. What else did he know about her? The old lady just nodded and smiled. Her button earrings caught the light.

She didn't laugh, but it was close. "This isn't someone you're fond of, I take it."

"Yes — no — we've just met —" Bernie tried to catch the blonde's eye, but she had wisely ducked behind a tall man. I could see her from where I was standing, but I wasn't about to say anything.

The lady handed the note back. "My Spanish isn't terribly good, or perhaps hers isn't. This part," she pointed to the words, "tells you to go back to the monkey house. That part calls you a fool."

Several people pretending not to listen snickered. Bernie said, distraught, "But the phone number — you don't give your phone number to someone you're calling a fool."

She smiled gently. "And I'll save you the trouble of calling it. The time now is eight fifty-three, and the temperature is about forty-nine." She turned away, and then I think she laughed.

Bernie turned back to me, dying hope in his eyes. "But why the silence? I don't get it. What'd I do to her?"

"Let's see that." Annie snatched it. She let out a single whoop. "Minnelang."

"What?"

"It was in the paper. It's an intensive language program at the U. of M. For a week you're not allowed to read, talk or speak English — just the language you want to learn."

Bernie looked from her to the note to the knot of people by the blonde. "What am I gonna do?"

I looked at him sympathetically. "Beats me, Bern. I've known you for years, and I never know what you're gonna do."

He slumped, a pathetic figure in rumpled sweats. Suddenly, before he could react, the blonde was back. She still had my pen. She passed it to me, did a double take at Bernie, took the pen back and wrote "Elizabeth" and another phone number on the bottom of the note.

She handed it to Bernie, hesitated, snatched it back and gave it to me, smiled at Bernie and left.

Bernie's like a kid; it only takes a little hope to bring the sun all the way back out in his life. "She likes me. See that?" He clouded again. "Why'd she give the note to you?"

"Safekeeping. Where are your pockets?"

"Right, right." He patted himself, then called to her, "Thanks. I'll keep it. But don't give it to Nate; he's not realiable. Anne, would you take it?" Then he looked Elizabeth full in the face and said shyly, "Um, *Gracias. Adios.*" His accent was terrible.

She didn't care. *"De nada. Adios."* And she was gone.

It was really a shame Bernie was so distracted; the movie was terrific. Harrison Ford's latest — I forget the damn title, but Annie was wild for him, and I was half out of my seat every third scene. They don't make heroes like that. Annie and I held hands like kids during the rough parts; I hope I didn't hurt her knuckles. It was terrific. Wish I could remember the title.

Chapter Thirteen

"Mr. Lowenbach?"

As early as I'd set out from the Twin Cities, still I was lucky to catch him at all. Even on Saturdays, Danny Lowenbach hit the office by eight-thirty. He lurched back from the car door, briefcase swinging ahead of him. Evidently it was pretty full; Danny Lowenbach took his work home.

"Yessir. Can I help you?" And he turned and looked at me and, dammit, I liked him. He had straight black hair that had just begun getting gray streaks; his tie wasn't straight and probably never would be, and he didn't look at all put out about taking extra time on a hurried morning. He was the kind of man who would stop and play with kids.

"I'm Nathan Phillips." Quickly as I'd put out my hand, he had his there quicker. "I wouldn't be surprised if you'd heard I was in town —"

"You know small towns, don't you?" He grinned. "Actually, I'm a stranger here myself. Only lived here nine years; you have to go at least twenty before you're a native."

"Uh-huh. Well, I'm asking a few questions about business people here for an investigation I'm doing. I wonder if I could talk to you this morning?"

He looked down at his briefcase and, on cue, his digital watch beeped. He tapped it with his other hand. "Sure. Not for more than half an hour, though. Gimme fifteen minutes to set up mail and messages?"

"I didn't think the mail came this early on — ?"

"Outgoing."

"Right." You wouldn't catch me going in this early on a Saturday unless I had to. Maybe that's why I can't afford a compact disk player. "Where's your office?" I already knew.

He told me and waved, dashing into his car and spinning tires as he left. Halfway down the block, he honked and waved at an elderly woman with a cane. She waved back until he turned the corner.

I waited until he was out of sight, then walked to his front door. It had been painted more recently than the rest of the house. Why? I scanned it carefully. The puttying job had been good, but if you looked closely you could still see the place where someone had filled in a small round hole, well above eye level.

BV Enterprises, Danny's office, was in the shadow of the B and V Granary. Most of the town would be, at sunset; as in most midwestern towns, the grain bins were the tallest buildings in town.

Danny's secretary wasn't in yet, or wasn't coming on Saturday, but she had a full desk to greet her. The coffee pot, on a timer from last night, was ready, and Danny was standing by his desk, talking on the phone. He waved me in when he saw me in the entryway. "Yeah. No, no problem. I figured if I called you now we could get our check cut by eleven, maybe drop by for yours to us by three-thirty. . . . Yeah, that's right; thank God for Saturday banking. Terrific. I'll see you later." He hung up. "Pull up a chair."

"Thanks. Do you want one?"

He looked around blankly at the wall, where there were oil paintings of field life, a map of Gordon County and an award from the Jaycees. "One what? Oh, chair. Thanks, I have one." But he stayed moving. "Coffee?" He saw me hesitate. "Half-caf. I cut it with decaffeinated; my stomach —"

"That's smart. I'd love a cup." I looked around dazedly. He had a tea table with leather chairs, one of those ultramodern streamlined office chairs with a joystick, even a backless kneeler like office furniture catalogues push for healthy people. None of them looked even remotely used. "Are you always this busy?"

"Huh?" I think he'd forgotten I was there. His nose was buried in yesterday's *Wall Street Journal*. "Oh. Look, I'm sorry. It calms down later in the day. I just like to get enough done so that I'm not asking Bernice to stand around on Monday, and so that if the boys drop in they have some work to look over. They do that some Saturdays."

Arlis's list had given me a good idea of who "the boys" were. "That doesn't look like a problem."

"Huh? Oh, sure." He grinned self-consciously. "There's always work around, but the moment you stop looking for it, it gets harder to find."

"I get what you mean."

He moved toward the chair, bounced away and began checking and filing folders. "What I mean is, you can look at work without seeing it, and it never gets done. Most people are pretty good at that. Ever notice how people won't see a sink full of dirty dishes until it's so jammed it's depressing?"

I nodded, a bit guiltily. "Or laundry."

"Or laundry, on the bedroom floor. Or dust, under the bed. Or a desk that needs straightening. Sometimes you find a thousand little things to do instead of your business." He shoved the file drawer shut firmly without slamming it. "Most of the guys that came to town the same time I did —"

"The Young Tigers."

That got a full grin. "You've been talking to the old guard, haven't you? Nobody calls them that any more, or thinks of them. Those guys could see the setup, and they could see the profits, but they couldn't see the day-to-day. It's a lot like the difference between a revolutionary and an administrator. Some people can start governments; other people can run them. When things get tough, the first kind do what revolutionaries are best at: they terrorize, they kill people, they control by force of personality. It's easier to see in Central America than it is in business." Now he was on the second drawer.

I was impressed. If it was self-knowledge, it was terrific; if it was knowledge of others, it wasn't bad. "So what happened to you?"

"Me. Right." And then he sat, barely on the edge of a chair. I've never seen a human being so uncomfortable staying in one place. "Let's say I've had a few horses shot out from under me." His mouth twisted wryly; then he looked me straight in the eye, frankly and unashamedly. "I started at a swimming-pool company. After all, farmers need fire insurance, and it means an on-hand supply of water, right?" He spread his hands. "One season. You can't convince a family farmer he needs a luxury more than he needs machinery.

"Next I started an ultra-modern poultry operation. Never was anything like it out here. It was beautiful; it had more hardware than NASA." He frowned. That one still hurt. "Know what it didn't have? Anybody that knew anything about chickens. Myself included. Two years, and I took too many people with me. There were some other projects, too." He flinched when I nodded. "Right. You've heard.

"After that I took a little time off and got a sense of myself. I was always looking for what wasn't here and trying to supply it. Maybe I oughta look at what was here, and improve it."

"The grain elevator."

"The B and V, right. Know what B and V stands for? Belle and View. It was a co-op that went under, and you can't take something totally away from a town like this without creating bad feelings. We gave former co-op members a storage discount, we took on the old debts — paid 'em off, too — and I learned never to ignore what's there." He stood up again. "We still do a lot of investing through this office, the futures market and options, but we work first in the present and with the no-option stuff. That's where you have to live."

I felt like a reporter doing a success-story feature. "Ever hear from those other guys?"

"Who? Oh, the other investors — the Tigers. You gotta remember, we were never close. It was a competition, to see who could pile up the most investment money from other people; we were more like Qaddafi than we were like other OPEC members." He smiled, thinly this time. "Maybe that's why I thought of the revolutionaries. They're off in Atlanta and Houston now, trying to stage financial coups. Some of them may do it. I saw a couple once, when I took a vacation a year or two back. They didn't think much of me. I guess from their view I've lost it." He shrugged. "I don't miss it. Now I'm in Rotary and the Chamber of Commerce, I nearly own my own house, and I have a business that'll be here even after I'm dead. None of them have that stuff."

I started to say something, then shook my head. "Mr. Lowenbach —"

"Danny."

"Okay. You're still half salesman, Danny; I came in to ask about the other people you're in with. What are they like?"

"Like? They're not; they're unlike. One runs a car lot, one ran an oil company he built from one gas station, one's a lawyer, one's a farmer, one's a druggist —" He ticked them off on his fingers. "Most of them have been in business longer than I have. Pretty sharp bunch. They keep me on my toes." He smiled, but he looked suddenly wary. "I don't like to talk about people behind their backs, though. Why do you ask?"

Maybe it was card-laying time. "Danny, one of those men tried to kill me. Another of them tried to contact my partner a couple of years ago, and my partner was set up and killed — by Stanley Colfax. You make it sound as though a couple of your co-investors are pretty experienced with cars."

That came as close to stopping him dead as anything could. "You're kidding."

"I'm not. My partner was smashed by a stock-car driver. Brian Frees was the contact man for that job."

"Frees —? Nah, you've got to be kidding me." He was too laughing, too earnest, overdone. "Not Brian. Hell, he's a rock in this town. I take him with me to church suppers, so people will think I'm respectable." But he knew.

"I know this is hard. I hate even to say it, but I'm sure he set up my partner. I know that because he murdered Stan Colfax." Now Frees could take me to court, if he wanted. He wouldn't.

"Colfax was killed by bees."

I needed Danny's information too badly to stop now. "And Frees set him up. Frees all but admitted it. He was working for a friend — someone he trusted, probably someone he's known all his life."

Danny Lowenbach was moving, but slowly, as though he were underwater or each step hurt. "God. You can't do this. You can't be right." He turned and looked bleakly at me. "Frees is one of my partners."

I felt a stab of pain behind my eyes. I was doing to him what Pederson and Annie had done to me, not too long ago. "I could still be wrong, but it doesn't look likely. If Frees worked with someone here, who would it be? Who does he trust?"

Danny leaned on his chair. For a moment I even thought he'd sit on it. Finally he said quietly, "Know anything about small towns?"

"A little."

"Not enough. A town this small, it's like family; you hate some people, you love a few others, but all of them you know better than you do your own heart. Better than people in cities can imagine. You wanna know who Frees knows well enough to trust?"

He was on the move again. "He was quarterback when Ed Parker was the Bee Vee Bombers' best wide receiver. I hear about the Chester game every time there's a board meeting. He worked summers for Niles Swenson, who got him drunk for the first time one Saturday at a farmers' bar. He bought land with Sammy Detweiler, and they go fishing at a lodge outside town — or used to; Sammy's not big on it any more. When Brian broke up with Karla Johnson, Virgil Keller went out with her — and when Karla broke up with him, they got together with Parker and a couple of other kids and jacked her dad's car up between two trees. I've heard that story twenty times, too." He spread his hands. "It's like a fraternity you can't join, because you weren't born into it. Brian wouldn't kill for any of them — you've got to be wrong — but he'd keep their secrets. Forever."

Danny was looking earnestly at me across the desk, his eyes wide and frank. He was trying to sell both of us.

"I hope you're right. Have any of your investors quarreled with each other?"

"Oh, yeah." He laughed uneasily. "Partners always quarrel. That's in the rules, I think. It's never come to blows as far as I now."

"Are any of them badly in the hole right now?"

The smile went crooked. "What's 'badly?' I've gone

under a time or two; is that bad enough? I don't think anyone's facing anything like that, but times are tough, and no mistake." A little Minnesotan was creeping into his voice. After nine years, you'd think it would feel at home there. "At least this business is sound. I overhaul the books myself" — he gestured at the computer in the corner — "and I have in a CPA every year to double-check. We're the soundest business in town." He coughed. "A couple of the guys have talked about selling their shares, putting money in other things, but no can do right now. No buyers. I don't think any of them are in trouble enough to get violent."

"Which ones would you say are in trouble at all?"

"Sorry, Nate. I don't feel like giving you any specifics." He looked me in the eye. "These men are the closest thing I've ever had to friends. If they have troubles, that's their business. If any of them come to me for help or . . . or anything else, that's mine."

He was a man to like. "Okay. I understand. Tell me, have any of them come to you for something else? To threaten you, or talk violence, or confess to something?"

Now he looked wary. "That's their business, too."

I gave my last shot. "Danny, don't shield this guy if you know who it is, or even if you're just guessing. He's committed two murders, and he's none too stable. If he knows I've talked to you, that makes you vulnerable. Even before I came, you were an easy target."

Danny didn't flinch, just kept moving slowly around the office. It was no wonder he stayed thin. "Then I'll talk to him. I get along with these people, Nate. I've committed my life to them now. I'm gonna fit in here, make something of myself and the community, something lasting. I've worked hard for them. That's got to count for something with them, and they count for me."

"Sure. Nice meeting you, Danny. See you around." Halfway to the door I turned. "Anybody ever tried to kill you?"

"Why do you ask?" But this time he flinched. Bingo. "Sheriff know?"

He was back in control. "I didn't say anyone did. Look, I'm sorry, but you'd better leave."

"Sure." I glanced at the computer again. "That's a great-looking machine. Some day I've gotta learn to use one."

"They're not hard. Save tons of time." He wasn't paying attention to me any more.

"Any of your partners know how to run it?"

"Oh, sure. Riley, and Parker, even Niles —" He swung his head back toward me. "Nice job. Get out." But he sounded sorry, and I felt sorry for him.

I went to the Crystal Café and had a late breakfast or an early lunch, this one alone. The hardest thing I ever did was sit down and stay there; the company you keep changes you, whether you want it to or not.

To the southwest there was a flat-topped hill, grass-covered and without boulders except on the side slopes. I stared around me, thinking how far this seemed from Danny's office.

Niles Swenson put another pinch of Copenhagen under his front teeth. "Glacial moraine. Years and years ago, when the glaciers came through, they melted here. And that's rocky, but it's the best soil in Minnesota. You see one of those on a farm, you know you have rocks, sure, but you have good soil."

I nodded. "Dad always said pound for pound the farm soil here was worth more than gold."

Swenson laughed. "Sure, sure. Used to be, anyhow. You don't look like a farmer, son."

"Never was." And never regretted it. "My dad was mostly dairy farming. If you've lived on one of those, you run away. I guess I waited too long to run." I watched the wind ripple through the drying grass stalks. "I never came back."

"You think maybe you were too smart?" He laughed again. Niles Swenson, all of sixty, looked like a county historical project. He had the droop-ended mustache of a Twenties Scandinavian — the kind of man the jokes call Scandihoovian, and some of the Scandihoovians do, too. His eyebrows were nearly as bushy as the mustache, and his brow and cheekbones were prominent in a thin, weathered but not dark face. The cords in his neck showed how much muscle he used to have, and he stood six feet plus in his steel-toed boots.

"Well, you sure didn't come out here to buy a farm. Did you? 'Cause I don't think I sell just yet."

"Wish I was buying. How much of this is yours?"

"Over to that stand of burr oaks, then south to the bottom of the moraine. West beyond the house clear over the hill" — it was a rise of maybe fifty feet, a hill only to prairie folk — "and back to that old barn you see there."

"Holy smoke." Farms always dropped my profanity back twenty years. "This is huge."

He nodded proudly. "And I'm not selling." He stared at me solemnly. "But what did you come out to ask, Mr. Phillips?"

"It can wait." This wasn't my man. My God, even agribusinesses didn't put together a spread like this. "I don't mean to sound naive, but this is one of the biggest farms I've ever seen. Can you see the whole thing anywhere but from here?"

"Oh, no. That's why I like this ridge. I walk out here when I want to talk." That was a reminder for me.

"You must be the richest farmer I've ever met." I tried to sound respectful instead of rude. I wanted his reaction.

He gave out several short, sharp laughs. "I bought it in pieces, when my neighbors got smart, and they quit farming. It sure took a while, you bet. But I'm not what you call rich, you know. I got to pay for this land every quarter. And I always do. 'Cause when I die, this farm goes to my children. That house there, it was built by my grandfather. This is a century farm."

I'd heard the term before: a farm the same family had owned and worked for a century. There weren't many of them. A year ago there had been more.

"Well, you know I've always made payments. They call me 'sir' at the bank." He nodded vigorously and looked me in the eye. Respect at the bank means a lot if you borrow for seed money.

It takes me a while. Niles was borrowing for more than seed money. I looked out over the land again. "One bad year can put a lot of this in danger."

He said sharply, "I've sure had two or three of those, and there's never been no danger. There won't be." He caught himself folding his arms, dropped them self-consciously. "I make every payment, and I pay off loans when I take them."

That was it. Land poor. It was more an Irish than a Scandinavian disease in the Midwest — the railroad builders and their children were tenant farmers long enough to resent renting — but some of the old guard Swedes and Norwegians had it too. You buy all the land you can afford, so you can see what you have. Then you go broke holding onto your wealth. If predictions were right and rural land prices kept dropping, Niles would become the richest-looking bankrupt in Gordon County.

Aloud I said, "Lucky for you. Some farmers don't have much land to put up for collateral, because of their mortgages."

He looked genuinely shocked. "I don't put up the land." He pointed to the south, even though Belle View was too far away to see. "I got some investments there. Lumber company, a building downtown, stuff like that. I borrow against those." He added, "Most years, the good ones I mean, I pay everything out of that and corn money." He winked. "Bean money goes to Yvonne an' me."

Now I was getting somewhere. "Mr. Swenson, here's where you get to throw me off your land. Or if you're in a good mood, you can simply refuse to answer." He chuckled, then spat tobacco juice. "Have you invested any with Danny Lowenbach?"

"Lowenbach!" He spat again, though he didn't need to, and wiped his mouth angrily. "Yah, sure, he talked me into some things." Like most people, when he was angry he talked like his parents had. "I betcha he's sorry he has my money. When he first come here, he talked about nothing but fast money and quick profits." Swenson's eyes glittered. Funny how some men who farm patiently season after season go a little wild at the thought of fast money. "Him and all his friends."

"The Young Tigers."

"Nobody calls them that now. They're all gone except for Danny Lowenbach." He curled his lip. "I put ten, twenty thousand dollars into his business. He makes it sound like it grows overnight. Then I come to him and ask, where's my profits? He shows me, and it's nice, but it's no gold rush, you bet. I say, you young sonnabitch, you promised a gold mine. You know what he says?"

Swenson jabbed me with his index finger, and I winced. He didn't notice. "He says, the gold rush didn't pan out. He's gonna stay and protect the investment, but it's gonna be a nice, slow, safe investment, like the other ones in town." He snorted. "If I wanted that, I'd put in with a friend. Sure, he's making money, but not the way he promised." His right hand was knotted into a fist, and I noticed for the first time how rough Swenson's hands were. Even at sixty, he'd be an ugly sparring partner.

"Wouldn't he give your money back?"

"Nah, nah. He said it wasn't fair to the other shareholders." Swenson's voice dripped scorn. "I say, they got their own problems. You give me my money. He says, look at the contract. He says, in five years he'll buy me out if the others won't. Till then, I can only get my forty thousand back by losing the profit."

Forty thousand? Niles had gone from ten to twenty to forty; I wondered which figure was a slip of the tongue. For now, I just nodded. "And he said you'd be helping the other partners by staying."

He said, too loudly, "Well, you know what I say? I say, hell with those other folks, let them get out if they want. I got plenty of safe businesses, if I wanted that."

Suddenly I sympathized with Danny Lowenbach. He should have cleared town when the rest of the Tigers had. Instead he was stuck pacifying and coaxing a group of bitter men dreaming of overnight riches. "But he never cheated you, or withheld profits?"

"Didn't I just tell you?" He snorted, a risky move when you're dipping snuff. "Every year I get my profit report, and he says plow my money back into the grain company. Sure, I do. But where's the big money? He does okay for a regular businessman, sure." He added sullenly, "He made us hire a CPA, to check his books, look over his computer. We even check the computer ourselves. The CPA said everything is fine. Yah, sure, fine. It's not his money tied there."

"Thanks for telling me, Mr. Swenson. I wanted to ask one of the investors how he thought Danny was doing."

Swenson looked at me sharply, and his hard face took on a mean edge. "You're investigating him?"

"Yah, sure." It was out before I could help it.

Swenson didn't notice. "Well, you look for everything, that's all. A man that talks like that, he has something wrong somewhere, you bet." He added bitterly, "We even bought him that office an' that fancy chair he never sits in. He just walks around that room like — like a chicken scratching. Never sits." Grudging respect came into his voice. "He works all the time like that, why doesn't he made fast money?"

"At least he works." Before Swenson could jump on me I said hastily, "There's one other reason I came out to talk to you. I hear your last fight with Danny was — well, bitter." I was giving him enough rope.

The last of the friendliness went out of his voice. "You been talking to Farrell?"

Nope. But let him think that. "Let's just say it's a matter of record."

"Nah, nah. If he said that, he's lying. Nobody charged me. I was never in court." He said it as though that made it all right. "I shot at him, sure. But I was never gonna hit him. If I wanted to hit him —" He shrugged. "Come back to the house." We walked, and he stared at the ground while we walked. "We fought in his office, sure, and I pounded that oak desk and said what I was gonna do to him. He didn't even shout back, just said it was law and I should be patient. I went back to the farm." He grinned. Smiles like that look normal on mean drunks, out of place on old farmers. "I got my thirty-thirty. That packs a punch, you bet. And I stood up in the vacant lot across the street from his house" — he stopped and put his hands up to hold an imaginary rifle — "and I held it just like this, and never even closed my left eye all the way." He squinted. "And I put a bullet three inches over his head in the front door.

"He ran in then, you bet. And after Farrell left I put one through his window, and in the wall one inch over his head. And then when he went to pull the shade, I put one an inch from his hand — one inch. Through the wood, so he'd know." He stooped over, picking up a beer bottle. "Damn kids." He set it on a fence post as we stepped over the top strand of barb wire.

"What happened then?"

He shrugged. "I went home. Farrell came out next

day." His voice shook. "He shook my hand, told me what a great shot I was. Said he wanted to see the rifle. He's a good shot, too, sure. I handed him the thirty-thirty, and he threw it in his car and said I could get it back in court but I might go to jail. Said his wife cooks good for prisoners, but I might not want that anyway." He sighed. "He gave it back before the last 'lection. Made me promise not to shoot Danny." Swenson turned defiantly to me, then started walking again. "Well, I haven't," he said, as if that were something to be ashamed of.

At the house he said, "You wait outside for a minute." I stood, arms folded. It was chilly in the shadows, even with a jacket. I looked back over where we had walked. The moraine was far in the distance; even the fence with the beer bottle was a good ways back. This was one hell of a farm.

Swenson stepped back through, rifle in hand. "You watch now." I watched, a hand near my jacket. At this range if he turned around and aimed at me I'd have plenty of time to draw. On the other hand, at this range he'd blow me back six feet if the bullet even touched me.

He didn't turn around. He didn't seem to know I was there. He raised the rifle easily, and when it was parallel to the ground it stopped as still as a tree branch on a calm day. He breathed softly, easily, and his right finger moved slowly and steadily. I barely saw the recoil.

The beer bottle on the fence post burst, the shattered pieces shining as they scattered in the sun. Swenson lowered the rifle. "You see?" He turned and walked back into the house, ignoring me.

I saw. If he'd wanted to kill Danny Lowenbach, he would have done it. And if he wanted to kill me, or Firebourne, or Frees, or someone else, that someone was going to die.

Chapter Fourteen

When the alarm went off, I jerked bolt upright, whacked the table instead of the button, hit the button on my next try and stared at the time. I moaned.

Annie said sleepily, "Huh? What? Oh. Nate. You all right?"

"Sorry. Why did I set the clock for six-thirty?" Especially, I might have thought — if I'd been capable of thinking — when I had stayed up till three.

"Six-thirty." Silhouetted against the window she looked leonine, hair ruffled every which way. "What . . . time is it?" We neither of us were too sharp.

I checked the clock again. "Still six-thirty. Today's Sunday, right? Why am I doing this?"

"Check your shoes."

"What?"

"Doesn't that work for men? If I check my shoes, I remember which pair I wanted. That tells me what I'm doing, sometimes."

"How many pairs of shoes do you own?"

"A closet full. Go look."

"I thought we were at my place."

"I mean, look at your *shoes*."

I stumbled out dubiously. Amazingly, it worked; I needed running shoes. "Bernie talked me into jogging, didn't he?"

Annie was prone again. "Yep," she said comfortably. "Told me you needed to get in shape and weren't fit to be seen naked."

"That's not true. I mean, it's not for me to say, but I've gotta be better than Bernie."

"Yep. I'd say so." She yawned. "Unless he looks a whole lot better naked. Nate?"

"Yes'm." I kissed her on the cheek.

"Don't call me ma'am. Do you have any coffee?"

"Colombian. And a coffeemaker. You getting up?"

"What are you, feeble?" At least it opened her eyes. "Put it where I can find it." And out she went and never said another word while I was there. The innocent sleep — I wonder if she was conscious at all.

I set the coffeemaker up and left a note saying so. After checking whether Marlowe was lurking to attack the note — not the first time he's been inconvenient — I tiptoed into the bedroom to find him sleeping in the blanket valley between Annie's ankles. I petted him, and he growled. Instead of being mad, I was tickled: he liked her after all and was guarding her.

Annie shifted, and he hissed at her. Nice guy.

I got to Bernie's by seven-fifteen. Bernie lives in a brick townhouse that looks like any other two-story condo from here to Cincinnati. Only the inside, the gadgets and the happy inmate set it apart.

So I wasn't too surprised when I pushed the doorbell and a synthesized voice said, "State your name."

I peered at the little speaker and the condenser mike over it. Another of Bernie's toys. "Gimme a break."

A bell sounded inside and the same voice announced,

using my own taped answer. " 'Gimme a break' is at the door." Nobody came running. I tried the door and to my surprise found it open.

That was because an elegant, remarkably pulled-together blonde in a Dior bathrobe was holding the other side of the knob. She smiled politely. "What did you say your name was?"

"Uh, I didn't. Nathan Phillips. Say, you're Elizabeth, aren't you? We met briefly at the, uh, the movies. You're speaking English," I added stupidly.

A laugh came and went behind the smile. "Now that I can. Bernie has said a great deal about you; won't you come in?"

As I did she said quickly, "Don't step on the robot."

I looked down. Something the size and shape of a vacuum cleaner with a tray on its back was bumping the carpeted steps repeatedly, sloshing the glasses of tomato juice on the tray. I edged aside. "Isn't science wonderful?"

"I wouldn't know." She leaned against the inside wall, hand on the banister. "I only know Bernie's version."

"Whozat?" Bernie leaned out of the bathroom at the top of the stairs, his hands covered with shaving cream. "Yo, Nate. Be with you in a minute." He turned back around.

I tried to look unrumpled and not hitch up my sweats. Elizabeth suddenly dimpled. "I'll hurry him up." She pulled that gorgeous blue robe up over her knees, dashed silently upstairs, then let go of the robe as her hands shot out and poked Bernie in the ribs, just as he was putting the cream on his face. "Whooooeeeeee!" And she was downstairs and gone, and all was silent except for the stubborn, tomato-soaked robot.

Bernie turned around, looking like a man who wants to shave his nose and eyebrows. "I don't understand her at all." Foam dropped off his nose as he spoke. "She'll go for hours, maybe days, perfectly normal, and then she'll just —" he gestured helplessly at his face, dabbing more foam on it by accident. "Gimme a minute."

I picked up a well-stirred half-full glass of tomato juice and sipped, accidentally leaning against the "repeat name" button on the inside end of the doorbell. "Gimme a break," I announced to myself.

Not more than half a mile down the road, Bernie and I decided we'd been athletic enough for one day. "So," I said while we waited in line at McDonald's, "how's it going?"

"Pretty well. How about you? Did Annie get home all right?"

"What kind of question is that? Minneapolis isn't that scary at night."

"Of course. You stay out late?"

" 'Fraid so. I didn't get much sleep." I said, partly to change the subject, "How's life with Elizabeth?"

Bernie hopped from foot to foot, bending his knees each time. Bernie could get part-time work as a stork.

"She's terrific, Nate. She's like nobody I've ever known. And she's — so right, you know?" He stared at me earnestly. "If she was a guy, she'd be me."

"You said she was right."

"No, I mean it. Well, maybe not me." He added with becoming modesty, "Better than me."

Now I was impressed. "And you're engaged."

"No."

"What?" I nearly stepped on his feet; now he had me hopping. We both looked like we needed a men's room. "Bernie, what's wrong with you? You ask someone to marry you if she has the right number of mouths."

He looked at his shoes as they appeared and disappeared under him. "Not yet. I want to be sure."

I picked up the tray. "Sure of what? My God, you're serious." Already? "So why not ask her? You've asked enough others."

He shook his head. "She's different. I can't just — Nate, she's too good."

"You think marrying you would cheapen her?"

"Nate, it's not funny. Don't you see? I've gotten engaged so fast, so many times . . . if I wait to ask her, she'll think I don't care; if I ask her, she'll think she doesn't mean any more than the others."

I thought about that and tried to remember that it wasn't funny. Only in Bernie's life would it make sense. "You could offer a prenuptial contract. That would be different."

"Sure, but she wouldn't know that. It'd look just like all those other times."

"Not to her. She wasn't there."

"But I was."

"This time you really mean it, don't you?" He nodded. "Then it really is too early to ask her."

He shrugged. "You'd always say that."

I didn't understand that, but I saw his problem. "Let me think."

We ate. Bernie was clearly carbo-loading for his first marathon. Two biscuits later I had an idea. "Offer to run off with her."

"What?"

"Elope, go to a J.P., hit city hall. She can't think you don't mean it then."

"What about the church?" Bernie's "the church" is Lutheran, Missouri synod.

"Afterward you can have a church wedding."

It took a minute, but he brightened. "Sure. Why, that'd be great. And you could be best man at city hall or wherever, and Dave could be in church — you don't mind, do you, Nate? I mean, it's just that you're not very religious."

"No, no, that's fine."

"And you'd still wear a tux at the wedding, but you could wear a suit at the civil wedding. You own a suit, don't you?"

"For God's sake, I'm not a bag lady."

"Just asking."

"Fine. If I didn't have a suit, I could wear my old prom dress. Listen, while you're just asking, why don't you go tell Elizabeth how you feel? Who know? Maybe she hates you."

"You think?"

"I was kidding. Tell her. Now."

"I could just call. Can I borrow a quarter?" He watched me fumble in my sweats. "I'll pay you back."

"Go."

"Right." Halfway to the door, he turned. "Can I ask you something?"

"Can I stop you?"

"How come you're so big on marriage all of a sudden?"

Then he left, running for once. But he's got no call to grin that way. I've always thought marriage was a pretty good thing.

My office was more than quiet. I read mail, realizing that I'd better get back to work or I wouldn't have a business. I'd had a good year, and I could afford to take time out, but unless this was going to be my vacation I'd be short of cash come Christmas. And I wanted to talk Annie into a joint vacation. I scribbled memos and sorted bills, trying to feel as industrious as Danny Lowenbach.

The door whispered open while I was paying bills. I said, "In a minute," then realized what a mistake that could be. Who knew I was in on a Sunday? I casually pulled my right drawer open; the spare Police Special was there. I had traded guns up in the past year, but kept the old one. I shifted the safety off, making sure it was loaded. "Okay, c'mon in."

My waiting-room door drifted ajar, then stopped. I raised the gun and lowered myself. The desk lamp between myself and the frosted glass in the door would hide any motion on my part. After some embarrassing incidents I'd meant to put a mirror in the dormer window so I could see who was out there. Maybe some day I would.

Thirty seconds later I said flatly, "Fun's over. In here slowly, hands in sight."

The door swung open and Sherri Christoff stepped forward slowly. "After all we meant to each other?" she said easily, but her voice shook. Sherri hates guns.

"Sherri. God, I'm sorry." I turned the gun away immediately, laid it gently on the desk top. "I wasn't expecting you." I added lamely, "But it's really great to see you."

"Hard to tell from this end." She shivered. "I was afraid to come in the moment you said, 'In a minute.' Nate, are you in trouble again?"

" 'Fraid so. Nothing big."

"That's a lie. You don't usually bring clients in at gunpoint."

"I hope you're not a client." Private eyes and dentists don't see happy people.

She shook her head, and I could see how much her hair had grown since I'd last seen her. "I was in the neighborhood and was hoping I could take a tough, cynical private eye to lunch. Is that a problem?"

I winced. Not all that long ago it had been; I couldn't go out in public and was afraid for my friends in private. Sherri, even though we had broken up, had put me up at her place when things got too rough for me to go home. "Really, everything's fine. I can handle this. It isn't even business." I bit my tongue on that one.

She only arched an eyebrow, something I'd always suspected she practiced. "No? I hope you haven't become your own client. Like you say."

She waited for my answer, and when I didn't have one she said abruptly, "Need to stay over?"

"No." I'd said it too quickly. Dammit, this was going to be difficult. "Nice offer, though."

She sat down. "Lunch can wait. What's bothering you?"

"Sherri, I'm going out with someone else."

She sat back. "So you figured on shooting me, now that you didn't love me any more? I don't buy that."

"No, that's something else, a murder investigation."

"You're pretty damn casual about murder." I had said that myself, years ago it seemed, in an argument with Jon. Back then he'd thought I was suppressing evidence. Now I was pushing an investigation Jon wasn't. Maybe you never could learn the rules.

"Hello? Nate? Anybody home?"

"Mmmh. Sorry."

"Don't tell me you were thinking about your new woman. Do you really have one, Nate?"

"I'm not sure." It beat talking business, suddenly. "I've met this really wonderful woman, Sherri. Her name's Annie, and she runs her own business — not some little shop, but an ad agency here in town — and she's self-reliant, and bright, and — she's even a feminist, and she —"

"My God." So much for her worrying about my health. "You're in love, aren't you? You're in love with a feminist, and it wasn't me."

"Waitaminnit. You were the one who broke up with me, remember?"

"Was I?" She had that look on her face that she had learned for blessing people out in Personnel at Dayton's. "Are you absolutely sure?"

"Almost. Are you sure it wasn't?"

"That's not the point." She hit the desk with the flat of her hand, and I jumped. "I can't believe it. Nate, you knew me for four years, and in all that time, you never so much as —"

I had one weapon left. "Sherri, will you marry me?"

"What? Are you crazy?"

"Let's say I am. Will you?"

"Of course not. That's not the point, either," She shook her head several times angrily. "Maybe it is."

"Sherri, I don't blame you for being mad. If you showed up with some clown on your arm and asked me to join you for lunch, I'd order double-cheese pizza and sling it on you. And I'd feel just as confused. Sherri, we've both gone out with other people."

Her answer, when it came, was surprisingly soft. Sherri doesn't speak softly much, not in that hurt tone. "I expected to fall in love first. That's all."

"I'm sorry."

"It's not your fault, Nate."

"Look, it's not your fault, either. You're lovable, and you've got high standards. Maybe you deserve better than you've met." I put out a hand and smiled. "I oughta know."

She squeezed my hand. "You were plenty good enough. You just weren't right." Her mouth quirked. "I guess I never thought that meant I wasn't right for you."

"It doesn't even mean that. You were perfectly right; you were just —" I groped for words. "Too damn tall."

"Too tall? Too *tall*? I'll kill you." But she looked better. "Let's go to lunch. I've had a rough weekend."

Ah. The opening I'd wanted, to get away from Annie without talking about business. "Personnel problems?"

"The worst. Do I usually run for company at lunch?"

"You can, any time. That doesn't change. Let's hear it, ace."

An hour later I knew all about how to fire and hire at Dayton's, and I'd put two glasses of wine down Sherri. At the end of the meal she could smile, and she wasn't up in the air about work. She even said she'd like to meet Annie some time. I said "Sure," but wondered if I could be out of town that night.

Willa had said Jon was at his office; it was quite the

weekend for business. In the outer office I said "Hi" to a
few of the guys I knew, to a pickpocket I'd met before on
business, and to Mike Olavsen. He'd just become a
sergeant. "Congratulations. So much for weekends off."

"What's a weekend?" He jerked his head toward Jon's
door. "Going in?"

"Sure, if he's not doing anything."

"Sometimes that's the worst time to interrupt him. Like
today." But Mike wasn't smiling. "Enjoy your talk."

When I entered, Jon didn't look up. "In a minute."

"Yes, sir." Just like one of his staff. It fooled him. He
nodded and grunted.

"Take a seat." Not a command, either. I hadn't seen
Jon with his subordinates much, except after a murder. He
had what my mother calls "a mouth on him" then; here I
could understand why young cops liked working for him.

I shifted the chair to the window — if he's been ques-
tioning someone, it's always in the corner, facing the blank
part of the wall — and stared out. Not much traffic. Not
much of a view, either.

I craned my neck to see over the pen-and-pencil set Willa
had given him and the can of advertising ball-points he actually wrote with. Jon was sorting his accumulated mail into the usual three piles: junk, do something about, do
something about but not now. The middle pile was grow-
ing.

He usually had it done by eight-thirty. Maybe he had
more mail than usual.

Jon poked the last letter in place and said, "Thanks for
waiting." He pushed his reading glasses up to look at me,
did a small double take, took them off. "Nate. I'm sorry."

"No problem. I'm no better than a cop."

"True, but you're not paid to wait for me."

"Consider me paid. I'm making my report." I cleared
my throat. "In Belle View yesterday —"

"You're fired."

"You don't pay enough for that."

"I'm doing it anyway." In the morning light he looked grayer than I'd expected — not just his hair; all of him. Finally, he said, "Okay, what happened?"

"Somebody tried to blow me up."

"You're still fired."

"I have to talk to Firebourne. He must know something, even if he wasn't as close to Colfax as Frees was."

Jon said, "You're guessing," but in spite of himself, he wanted to know what I'd guessed.

I gave him a chance to ask. When he didn't take the bait, I said, "Colfax moved in near Frees. If Colfax had been blackmailing Firebourne, he'd have moved there. When a man's in your pocket, you keep an eye on him."

Jon only said, "Maybe." He wasn't nearly as interested as I wanted him to be.

I said casually, "When we drive back down —"

"I said you were fired. I'm fired, too."

It took me a second. "You're leaving a murder open?"

"No, I'm not. Colfax is dead. Couldn't be tried again anyway. Frees did nothing we can prove."

"Somebody did."

"Not in Minneapolis."

I said it as gently as he would to the kids that worked for him. "We've started things rolling."

"And if we leave them, they'll stop." There was nothing to say to that. He sorted the pile he'd already sorted and sealed a return envelope. He didn't look hurried, and he didn't look happy.

Finally I said, "I'm not quitting."

He stopped, then picked up another letter, read it and tossed it aside. "Good luck."

He looked straight at me. That part of his job I'd seen before: the flat, blue-eyed Scandinavian stare that makes rookies wish they were dead and buried somewhere in another town. "All my life I've come in after crimes and picked up the pieces. Sometimes, when I was real lucky, I could stop a crime. Maybe even a murder. I don't ever start them.''

He pushed at his mail. He might do it all morning, unless something came up. "This place, this Belle View, was different. Nate, we caused a death — maybe not pulling triggers ourselves, or strangling Colfax with our bare hands, but the result was the same." He caught my eye. "Okay, somebody had it in for Colfax before we got there; maybe we only hurried things up. I still don't like it, Nate. If I have to kill innocent people to get some law —''

"Colfax wasn't innocent, and we didn't cause his death." But I knew Jon's answers before he said them.

"Maybe Colfax was guilty; we were never sure. But he wasn't guilty, either; not by law. And I don't wear a judge's robes." He looked somber. "The toughest part of this job is, I have to take the kids I've been busting my butt to make cynical and cautious and tired and distrustful, and I've got to convince them the oath still means something. Maybe it doesn't." He opened his hands. "I don't know about the death penalty, but I'm damn sure people shouldn't apply it themselves, out in the streets. That's not their job. It's not mine, either.''

"Sometimes it's your job to finish things you start.''

"I don't think so. Like I said, I fired myself. I'd fire you, too, if you'd let me.''

I shook my head. "You like old movies? 'When a man's partner dies, he's supposed to do something.' ''

Different things flickered across his face when I said that: pity for me, shame at what he'd done and what he wouldn't do, fear for my life. "Sometimes there's nothing good to do. Maybe you can do something — maybe the people who pulled the strings on Roy's death are still out there — but I don't want to be the one that gives them what they deserve. I wouldn't like to see you be that one, either.''

I stood up. "I'd better get back there.''

Jon nodded. "Door's that way. I'll do anything I can for you, but don't expect much help. I arrest people. I don't hunt them down." Then he stood up. He'd never stood to see me out before. Maybe he thought I was a rookie. "Stay safe, and stay careful. I've been at this a long time. You know what I see, when I look around that town there? A whole mess of insects, crawling all over dead men. It's like that. They don't mean any more harm than you do, maybe."

At the car, Annie asked if everything was okay. I said Jon wasn't going with me. She acted like nothing had happened, but in the next ten minutes she asked me if I was all right maybe three times. She didn't seem to like my answer.

I managed to get out and say goodbye without bringing up business, but I could see our lives would get awkward unless I wrapped up work in Belle View soon. What the hell. I drove back down, booked a room at the Harvest Hotel, and lay down to nap before supper. There was something secure about being here, knowing that no one was aware I was in town. I drifted off, feeling perfectly safe.

I needed sleep more badly than I'd thought; it was dark when I woke up. I was wrong about no one knowing, too: the phone was ringing.

Chapter Fifteen

"What?" I wasn't at my sharpest. I hadn't been sleeping well, and after supper these days I didn't react quickly. "I mean, hello?"

"Go to Firebournes'," The voice had said simply, and hung up. I couldn't identify it, but that wasn't surprising.

So I went to Emil Firebourne's — after calling Josh Farrell and saying I was headed out there. I told him about the call.

"Who knew you were down here on Sunday?"

"Nobody in particular. Anybody that checked at the desk, or knew my car."

"Don't go."

"Why not?" But I knew.

"Because this sounds like a setup. You want to die?"

"Some day. Not yet. See you there."

I pulled into Emil's lane clumsily, clutching the steering wheel with one hand, my thirty-eight with the other. Lately people in the gun business had been trying to convince me to switch to a .357 Magnum. Most of the time I didn't want to carry that much firepower.

I felt marginally better when I saw how many cars were already there.

Suddenly red lights flashed in my rearview mirror, closing fast. Farrell? I pulled over as far as possible, setting my gun on the seat. Maybe it wasn't Farrell, and anyway a badge doesn't always make a man honest.

It wasn't Farrell, but it wasn't a problem: an ambulance tore by, rocking from side to side on the gravel. I followed more slowly. I wasn't used to rutty gravel any more.

I passed the barn and corral on the right. Emil's horses, huge Clydesdales that probably weighed more than Honda Civics, were watching curiously, disturbed by the siren. By the mercury-vapor yard light they looked like huge, dark blocks, mostly shadow and strength. The way they watched made me think of a story a German immigrant used to scare the bejeezes out of me with when I was a kid: "The horses of Death," he said, "are made of weight and darkness. When you are dying they come and watch, to see you don't get up." Nice thing to tell a kid. I put my gun back into my jacket pocket and parked.

Then it registered: horses walk around by themselves, but they don't open barn doors. Somebody, maybe everybody, was in the barn.

I glanced up at the loft. Sure enough, there were silhouettes in it, backlit, on either side of the track for lifting bales. I vaulted the corral fence and dashed to the side of the building, waiting for shots.

There weren't any. I put my ear to the weathered boards, but they were too thick, the cracks too narrow. I edged to the open barn door, hoping my motion wouldn't stir the Clydesdales. Big as they were, they wouldn't hurt me, but anyone inside could tell that someone had stirred them up.

As I got closer, I heard muttering. Nobody was trying to

hide — with all the cars here, no one could. I stood a moment at the door's edge, peering around.

Then I put my gun away and walked in. Nobody was looking, except Ada.

She wasn't likely to see me. I hadn't known who she was at first; her feet were twisting back and forth at eye level. She was in a faded print dress, probably kitchen clothes. People were shy about looking up too close under her. She had on a small gold chain necklace that contrasted strangely with the horse reins she was dangling from.

The ambulance crew was in the loft — they were the ones I'd seen before — arguing softly about cutting her down or waiting for the sheriff. "We can't do anything for her. We could be destroying evidence." "You don't give up till you gotta. CPR could —" "For pity's sake, Mark, she's stone cold!" He said it more loudly than he wanted to and then looked around guiltily. Nobody paid any attention.

I tried to do what Jon would have done — note every detail, writing them down if I had to. I pulled out my pocket notebook, the one that mostly gets doodles, and sketched the layout in case they did take her down. I wrote: "Arms free, swinging at sides. Reins tied to crossbeam over loft. Crossbeam reachable for her from stool in loft. Hay dislodged from edge of loft floor, corresponds to clump on barn floor under her feet. Angle of neck suggests death by broken —" I scratched that out. The coroner would do that, and better.

"Extra set of reins dangling from the edge of the loft; free end hangs down maybe six or seven feet. No signs of a struggle." I shut the book as the men upstairs lowered the body. I went forward to help catch it, but I was too late. Niles Swenson and Brian Frees had caught her, and Virgil Keller had his bull's arms wrapped around Emil, who was struggling and crying, "Easy — easy! For God's sake, don't hurt her —"

I looked around. This place was a who's who of the people I'd met and had wanted to meet: Keller, Swenson, and

Frees, all looking more miserable and scared than when I'd seen them before; a man I recognized as Kevin Riley from the grinning ads for Riley Rambler; a man he called Pat, who looked half like a lawyer and half lost. That would be Pat Cavanaugh. The others I wasn't as sure of. I wondered if they'd all gotten calls like mine, and who had done the calling.

Farrell said, behind me, "Tried to talk to Emil?"

I turned around. "Who could?" I showed him the sketch. "I'll help with the report. They took her down."

He glanced around. "Maybe none of these folks knew better." I didn't like his tone.

"They thought there was a chance she was alive —"

"Not a chance in hell. What you want to bet somebody besides the ambulance crew mentioned that idea first?" I shut my mouth. Farrell was way ahead of me. "And nobody's gonna agree on which one said it. And what's it matter? She hanged herself, didn't she?"

"No," I said softly.

"No," he agreed. "Don't leave yet." He walked over to Emil. "Emil, I gotta talk to you; I'm sorry."

Emil nodded dumbly, not taking his eyes off the men who were looking over his wife. CPR had stopped; evidently her neck was broken. Emil's mouth hung slack, the gold fillings in his front teeth catching the light. Even at a time like this they were hard to ignore.

"These are tough questions just now. I hate like hell to ask them." He cleared his throat. "Was Ada depressed?"

Firebourne shook his head slowly. "She was real worried about her sister in California, but that's all. Twyla has cancer, and Ada is — was scared it runs in the family." He shook his head. "But not this scared."

"And when did you see her last?"

"After supper. She came down here to toss trash to the pigs. We do that, y'know," he said earnestly. "But just vegetable trash, no meat. I don't see why she came to the barn, though."

"Right. Emil, did you and she have any words? About money worries, say? Or fights about anything else?" I hadn't known a man that big could sound that gentle.

"Not a bit." That he was firm on. "Just look at this place. We're set." He looked around again, confused. "Everything was going so good —" His gold fillings were showing again.

"That's enough for now, Emil. I'll talk to you tomorrow or the next day." He turned around, then turned back. "Oh, sorry. One more. She leave a note?"

Emil handed him an already-crumpled sheet of paper that I hadn't noticed in Emil's right hand. I read it around Farrell's arm — I couldn't see over his shoulder: "Love you. Ada."

Farrell said slowly, "I want to keep this, Emil, but I promise you, you can get it back. I'll take real good care of it." He added, "If you gotta see it, call and I'll come out."

Emil only stared, at Farrell as much as at anything. Pat Cavanaugh walked up to him tentatively, put an arm on him. "I think you oughta go back to the house, Emil." Firebourne led the way, but Pat looked less of a blind man than Emil did.

Farrell looked around. "What are the rest of you doing here?" He didn't seem to expect an answer.

Niles said quickly, "Emil called me. I called Pat, and he called the ambulance."

"Uh-huh." Farrell walked around the barn, reading the stall signs. You could park a car in stalls that big. "Who called Danny?"

After a moment's silence, Niles said, "I think Emil did."

"Right." Farrell spun around. "And if you boys are all here, where in the hell *is* Danny Lowenbach?" I hadn't until then realized what I should have long ago: these men were the major investors in Danny's company, the men who were working together and slipping out from under him.

They shuffled, like kids asked an awkward question. Finally a man who, by a process of elimination, had to be Sammy Detweiler said flatly, "Some things we do without Danny, Josh. He don't run us any more."

Farrell snorted. "If he'd been here, there'd been less milling around and more sense."

Niles said loudly, "Things change, Josh. I don't think you'll see Danny out to my place any more."

"Maybe I should take your gun away again?" Farrell was quiet, but suddenly his hand was on his hip. I moved, I hoped unobtrusively, to one side, ready to cover the others — and felt crazy. What was this, the OK Corral?

After a moment, Niles shrugged and smiled under that droopy, old-country mustache. "If you want, Josh." He held his hands away from his sides. "I got it with me, in the car." He grinned. "I didn't always get on so good with Emil, either."

"I remember." Farrell relaxed, then turned to me. "Let's leave this place to Emil's friends. They'll do him more good than we can."

"Sure." I looked directly at Frees; he wouldn't meet my eyes. He was careful not to look at anyone else. Smart man.

Outside, Farrell lit a Camel and sighed. "These damn things. I'll never quit 'em. I've tried." He added, conversationally, "Thanks for in there. This bunch doesn't need that, though."

I didn't realize I'd been that obvious. "You think not?"

"Nah. No nerve. By the way, you look like hell. Have you tried sleeping?"

"Recently, not much. Listen, they need more watching than you think."

"You know something I don't?"

"Ada Firebourne didn't kill herself."

"Emil'd be glad to know that, I think. Might mean some insurance, too, long as he didn't do it. By the way, you think that's news?"

"No. But it's obvious."

"Let's hear your reasons."

I watched the horses shift in the corral. "One: generally, people who hang themselves don't wear necklaces. Silly, but there it is: they're afraid the rope or whatever will catch the jewelry. A lot of them don't wear earrings, either." Farrell just watched me.

"Two: the hay on the barn floor. If she got up on that stool to reach the crossbeam, she'd have jumped from there. If you hang yourself, you want the largest drop you can come up with. Someone else tied it, and then she was pushed."

"And she didn't struggle, what with both hands free."

"Nobody said she had both hands free. Three: there was more rein hanging over the loft edge. Whoever hanged her looped that around her hands, probably behind her back, and spun it unlooped just after she died. If there was any time between her death and finding her, the blood settling in her limbs would hide any marks."

Farrell glanced back toward the barn. "Why not just knock her on the head, or choke her? Seems like less trouble."

"It also seems like more marks. You'd have to make sure she scraped her head over the head knock as you dropped her. That would be even less realistic; suicides generally leap high and far. As for suffocating, you could do it with the reins and it wouldn't show, but you'd need a lot of luck for the victim not to bruise herself while she fought for air." I grimaced. Everything I said made this fake suicide less tidy, more real. "How'm I doing?"

"You got it all. Left out one thing."

"Who did it."

"S'right. And the smart money says it was one of the boys that showed up tonight." He sighed. "I've talked to Danny Lowenbach about this bunch, but he won't say word one. Maybe he doesn't know which one is cutting rough, but I think he's guessed."

"I talked to him, too. I think he's trying not to find out."

We were at Farrell's car. He put a hand on the door. "Know what else? I wouldn't give a pitcher of warm spit for his life if he looks around much." He looked at me hard. "Or if you do."

Even though it was chilly, I left with the windows rolled down, listening for anything. All I heard were massive horses shifting in the shadows.

Chapter Sixteen

On Monday, I got lost going back out to Frees's place. Maybe that was psychological; it wasn't one of my favorite places.

I decided against parking down the road and sneaking up on the place again. It wasn't likely he was going to shoot me on sight, but I was getting nervous in and around Belle View. Maybe I needed more sleep.

The trees in the windbreak were losing leaves rapidly; you could pick out the pines easily. The black walnuts were long bare, last trees to get leaves and first to lose them. His lawn was nearly leaf-free. Maybe Arlis Schmidt could have found fault with it, but I couldn't.

He wasn't in sight. I pounded on the door — no answer. I got that itchy feeling in the small of my back that I get when someone I don't trust could be anywhere: behind me, above me, out to the side waiting for me to drop my hands.

I pounded on the door again and listened. Nothing from the house, but from the back came a rhythmic brushing sound. I tiptoed, then abandoned it and walked almost normally.

Brian Frees was in back, pipe in mouth, raking leaves off the very spot where Colfax had died. A little girl, blonde and very energetic, was hopping from one big root to the next. I wanted her to move.

The girl didn't pay any attention to me. Frees looked up when he heard me scuffing through the leaves. "Hello, Nate." That was it. He went back to raking.

I said. "Quite a job."

He looked around. "Yah, yah. Section over by the house is done, though." He pointed with his pipe. "All since this morning. Kathy! Don't wander off, now."

The blonde, walking a doll ahead of her, was going toward the east fenceline. She came bounding back, smiling wider than grown-ups can or will.

"Lot of energy there. Too bad you can't harness it for the leaves."

"Oh, she's a great help," he said solemnly. "Kathy! I want you to meet Mr. Nathan Phillips. What do you say?"

"Hi, Mr. Phillips," she said shyly.

I shook her hand, then shook hands with her doll. "And this is —"

"Gloria."

"Hello, Gloria."

Kathy swayed back and forth on stiff legs, then bounded away. Her standing-still quotient was not high.

"My wife's niece — youngest niece," Frees said, satisfaction in his voice. "Every so often she comes here for lunch and a sandwich, and to help out with the yard work."

I nodded. "Looks big for four." If she'd been five, she'd be in school this morning.

"Nearly five. They held her out of preschool; figured she was shy." He shook his head. "Next year she'll run that place."

We watched her together. It upset me, how at peace he was, but I could understand his enjoying Kathy's visits. She ran back towards us, and simultaneously I heard scuffling far behind us.

It stopped before I turned around. From the sound, it had been near the leaf pile, two or three feet high, that Frees had already gathered in the corner. Frees looked where I'd looked. "Coon, probably. Or something smaller; even a sparrow makes a whee of a sound on leaves." He looked down at Kathy. "But it could be Mr. Humpty the Bear again."

She laughed up at him. "There's no bear!" She flapped her arms out from her sides; laughing took all of her.

"Well, no. At least, not many bears." He cleared his throat. "But you remember Humpty."

She dropped Gloria and sat, leaning the doll against her side. "You remember last time I told you how Humpty had bought some roller skates —"

I took the rake from his unresisting hands. I'm not much for lawn work, but it felt good, on a crisp fall day, to do a little. I tried not to think what else I'd seen on this lawn.

After Frees had taken Humpty the Bear around a skating rink, into the street, and rolling out of control down Highway 63, Kathy hugged him and ran off. He took the rake back. "You didn't have to do that." His eyes were troubled.

"No problem." I wasn't sure why I had. I think I was missing farms and lawns.

He glanced toward Kathy. "She'll play by herself a while now. What is it you wanted to ask?"

"I just wanted to say something." I watched as he smoothly and efficiently raked leaves onto a canvas carrier.

"Say away. Better hurry; she won't stay away long on just one story." He added, "Thanks," as I helped bunch the corners of the canvas so he could drag it, leaf-jammed, to the pile.

"I know you killed Colfax. Maybe you just helped him kill himself; that would put you out of reach. If you did dump a bee on him — and I'm betting you did; otherwise you left too much to chance — then we could get you if we could prove that. You know we can't."

He shrugged. "I don't know much about police work." He avoided my eyes.

"Chances are Colfax got paroled earlier than you expected and put the bite on you. It sure looks that way."

"Can't say as I follow you there." He walked back for another pile.

"Which he could only do if you hired him to kill Roy Cartley."

If he'd said "Who?" I might have hit him. He didn't even look my way. "So you're saying I killed Colfax to hide killing this Cartley. Ain't that a little like burning down a town to hide arson?"

"If it's clumsy, sure. Not the best idea, even if you're careful. But I don't think it was your idea."

That brought him up short. "Why not?" He tried to smile. Bullseye. "Don't think I'm bright enough?"

"Not exactly." He looked offended. "I can't figure out yet why you'd want to kill anybody. No, I'm looking for somebody else. My bet is that I'll find someone — a neighbor, a good friend, probably both — and it'll turn out that he pushed you into it. I think that same person killed Ada — don't try to tell me that was suicide. And when I find that person, you'll talk. You'll have to."

He opened his mouth, shut it. "Not as much as you talk."

Together we hauled the last bundle of leaves over to the pile. "Thanks," he said briefly, and added, "What you said doesn't make much sense to me. Maybe you'd better think it through again." He looked me straight in the eye, and I knew he'd stick to his story no matter what I said. He called, "Kathy."

Kathy was sitting on the far side of the yard. She'd set Gloria on a rusty coffee can, put a bucket between them, and was squatting there serving imaginary tea. She picked up Gloria and bounced over.

She grabbed Frees at kneecap level and squeezed; he nearly toppled. "Oh, now. I wanted to give you a last chance at jumping in the leaves. Can't do it after it's lit."

She ran to the pile, stopped in front of the near edge and jumped two or three feet, dropping back on the seat of her pants. The leaves shifted, but stayed piled. She ran out and did it again.

"That's enough," Frees said after the third time, and she stood back. "Now watch."

He took matches from his shirt pocket. After two tries a tiny flame moved west across the leaves. There was no wind at all. Kathy stood, fascinated, within a foot of the pile, watching as the flames turned four inches high, then six, then nearly a foot, dancing forward and leaving ashes behind them. Behind the flames, the ashes puffed and settled.

Frees and I stared, too. Something about fire draws the eyes, seems magic. What was bulky and alive one minute is small and insubstantial the next. The piled leaves near the fence sighed and settled into the flames, driving them higher. We were so entranced we barely noticed as they uncovered a single, bright-red gas can.

Small as she was, I doubt if I hit Kathy much over her waist, diving between her and the fire and trying not to look over my shoulder. I'd stooped too low diving; I stumbled. I wrapped my arms around her and kept rolling east, fast and hard. She gave a first frightened cry, but there was no time to worry about being gentle. I was five feet from the fire. Eight. Fourteen.

A sudden hungry roar rushed to meet me; I felt the first heat. Even facing away, I caught the reflection on the grass. Still rolling, I opened one eye. No sense losing both.

There was a column of flame fifteen feet high, arching —
falling —

I rolled, dug my feet in and did clumsy somersaults.
Eighteen feet. Twenty-five. Kathy was shouting for Uncle
Brian, and he was running our way.

The flaming gas splashed down not four feet behind me.
I stood and ran, crashed straight into Frees. I looked at
him, wild-eyed, and clutched Kathy with one hand while I
swung with the other.

He caught my fist. "Give her here," he said, and his
panic was no small thing. "Give her here. Please."

Kathy launched herself into his stomach with a sob, and
he caught her, pulled her to his chest, held her. "It's all
right. You'll be fine. Nobody got hurt."

The blaze was spreading across the lawn, but slowly; it
hadn't been that dry a fall. I took a deep, shaky breath.
"Got a hose?"

"Side of the house. No, no, other side." I hadn't
wanted to go to the west side. That was where I'd hidden in
the trees, proving that someone else could do it, too. This
morning someone had; someone stealthy enough to walk
within twenty feet of me without my hearing. Once out of
Kathy's sight I took my gun out.

Nobody was there. I heard a car start up and dashed
through the windbreak. There was too much dust for me
even to guess at the car color, let alone the make or license.

I came back with the hose spraying. The fire was out
within five minutes; the gas had burned itself out almost
immediately, leaving only grass and stray leaves blazing. I
hesitated, then sprayed what was left of the pile of leaves.
What if there was another can somewhere?

Frees walked up and took the hose. "I'll soak her down,
now. Thanks. You did good, Nathan." His voice was still
shaky. "Oh, God, she coulda died. Little Kathy, dead, and
all because —" He stopped.

"Because of what?" I kept quiet, and glanced back at

Kathy on the stoop. She had a fingerlock on Gloria; all through that chaos, she hadn't let go. "Seems it's pretty important."

"It is. Never mind." He ran a hand up where his hair used to be.

I looked at the charred fence post, the smoking grass. "Your buddy is crazy. He didn't get you this time, but he will. And after all this, you want to protect him."

"It's not like you're thinkin'." He stamped out a smoldering clump near our feet.

He looked wide-eyed and afraid, and for the first time since I'd known him he sounded defeated.

Any sympathy I'd had for him was fading fast. "Fine. If you don't like what I think, talk to somebody else. Dig up Colfax and ask him. Check with Ada in the morgue, and tell her to save room for Kathy."

That snapped his head up. I went on, "Maybe you don't think Kathy's involved. She wasn't, until she nearly died. I guess Kathy's mother trusts you the way you trust the man who did this; think about that, and keep away from your relatives until —" I swallowed. Until whom? "Until your buddy with the gas can is dead. I wouldn't talk to Emil Firebourne, either, if I were you. That man has death written on him in big letters." I stopped for breath, and realized that my next step was to talk to Emil myself. I didn't sound too smart, either.

He called as I left the yard, "I won't forget this. I'll do what I can for you."

That stopped me. I turned towards him. "As much as you did for Ada Firebourne? You're the one that called me." After a second, his head jerked imperceptibly. It wasn't an admission of guilt, but at least it was something. "Thanks. Did her a lot of good, didn't it?" I tried not to think about what his last words meant as I walked to the car.

I called Emil, but nobody was home. Maybe he was with

Farrell. I didn't do much more than walk around in the afternoon; little that I said made sense and less stuck with me. Sooner or later I had to get some sleep. Maybe I should take tonight off.

So I was pretty happy when Annie showed up at the Harvest Hotel. "Nate." She ran across and pecked me on the cheek. "I hope I'm not ruining your plans."

"Ruining my plans, answering my prayers, that sort of thing." I thanked God the skinny-necked clerk wasn't on duty; nobody should have to see that smirk. The woman, probably his wife, just smiled. "Staying the night?"

"Yep. Brought my own car; I have to leave for work tomorrow. Seriously, will I be in the way?"

"Hope so. Take you to dinner?" And that was that. Part of me was afraid, sorry she came down where she could be seen with me, where she was vulnerable. Sooner or later I'd have to break the rules and tell her what was happening here. I didn't want to.

During dinner, I called Emil's again. Still no answer. I was relieved for Annie's safety, but annoyed at the delay.

After dinner we went straight back to the Harvest Hotel. I'd had tea after dinner, hoping it would keep me awake enough to talk. Once we were in our room, Annie said, "You look exhausted. Want to sleep? I said sleep."

"Yeah, but no." I fumbled. "Annie —"

I shut up as the lights in the room went out. I searched frantically for my gun, which I'd left on the dresser, but calmed down when Annie said, looking out the window, "Power outage. Every light in town is out." She added, "Sure you don't want that sleep?"

"Positive." I was glad she hadn't seen my face the moment before; it would have wrecked the mood. That power outage couldn't have been better timed.

We sat together in the dark, enjoying an anticipatory silence. Finally Annie said, a little breathlessly, "Nice sunset."

I said, "Yeah." I didn't care if there were two suns. I

took off my watch, did a double take, and suddenly I cared. I stood up and stared out the window.

Annie, with admirable restraint, only said, "Something interesting?"

I put on my jacket and grabbed my watch cap. "Sunset was an hour ago."

She stared into the rosy light on the horizon. "Then what's —"

"Fire. Lots of it. Here." I put the gun in her hand. "If anyone but me tries to come in, shoot them. Be careful, okay?"

She said, "Sure. Can't I come with you?"

I thought of Kathy, playing within inches of an explosion. "You'd be safer shooting me. I'm not your boss, but I wish you'd stay here."

Bless her, she said, "Will do." She stared at the gun, too confused to tell me to be careful, or else she knew it wasn't much use. I was headed for the largest fire either of us had ever seen.

Chapter Seventeen

Even between stores in the alley you could tell something was wrong: too many shadows and patches the wrong color to come from street lights or even anti-crime lights. Sparrows and chickadees flew restlessly around the downspouts and the doorsills; the false dawn confused them. This far away, the smoke was nothing but a faint pervasive smell, just enough to bother the animal in me. Nothing in town would sleep well tonight.

I parked three blocks away. I wouldn't be the only watcher, and I didn't trust a fire in a town full of frame houses. I almost pulled back further; from three blocks you could see the tops of the flames, and the people running toward them cast huge, sharp shadows. Even in silhouette they moved agitatedly, unnaturally, like out-of-control puppets.

At first I thought I was just excited; the roaring in my ears could have been my pulse with high blood pressure back of it. I yawned, swallowed, then realized: that fire made enough sound pressure to be uncomfortable. I pulled my watch cap over my ears. That helped some.

Now I wasn't alone. The last time Belle View had had this many people in the streets was probably the Harvest Parade. Then, at least, they were happy. I looked around, not recognizing many faces, and realized that at least one of them was probably the killer I was looking for. My hand went to my pocket uselessly; I had more sense than to take a gun and bullets to a fire. Maybe he'd be too busy to bother with me.

At one block I unbuttoned my jacket. Even from the far sidewalk, looking over Denton's Farm Fleet, you could see more flame than building. Something, probably the heat, had set off the railroad crossing signals; over the fire you could hear the bells. Nobody paid attention to them.

I stood and stared by the sawhorses in the middle of the street. If the killer was near, this was his chance.

The grain bins themselves looked huge from here, tall enough to seem like they were leaning overhead. When I was a kid, I used to stand under bins like that, watching the clouds pass and pretending the tops of the bins were falling forward. But these bins were five stories of grain bin plus three stories of flame, monsters that made the Statue of Liberty torch look like a kitchen match.

The roofs were long gone. The corrugated metal sides glowed red at the top rims. Sparks shot straight up and disappeared, propelled by the roaring air. In the center of the twisting, impossibly huge flames was a straight column so bright it almost hurt to watch.

I ducked sideways as somebody shoved on me. A man in a John Deere jacket shouted in my ear, "Grab that end!" and motioned. I picked up the left end of the sawhorse and carried it aside as another fire truck careened in. I hadn't even heard the siren.

I looked at the parking lot below the granary. It was an effort not to stare back into the flames. Three fire trucks stood at their separate hydrants; the fourth moved to the far corner of the bins and disappeared. At least the town county was prepared for fires.

Prepared, maybe; ready, never. No one could be ready for a fire this size. I was at Walnut Grove when they demonstrated a fifteen-pound fire hose by rolling a key the length of a block with the water pressure. Five hoses that big were already playing across the bins, making a lot of steam but no other visible difference.

A man in a black fireman's slicker ran up to the barrier. "You and you." I didn't ask if I was "you," just ducked under. "Grab a ladder and follow me."

"Fine." We did. The other man was a head taller than I and twice my width; he was easy to keep up with and carried more than his share of the weight. The fireman, axe in hand, gestured us close to the bins and pointed beyond.

"Jack-and-Jill store?" shouted the big man. The fireman nodded. "Well, hell."

We stopped a second. "Mind cutting close to the fire?" He looked tired under the fire helmet; sweat streaked the soot on his face.

We said we didn't. "Watch it," he said simply, and trotted off. We stepped over hoses, debris and some twisted metal; I wished I had boots on.

At our closest point to the granary the big man looked up, then ducked down. I heard it then, and looked: a section of sidewall, half red, half blackened and the size of a storefront, wavered over us. There was nowhere to run. I ducked and kept on lugging the ladder. Stupid way to die.

It fell in, not out, disturbing the air column of the fire. Suddenly we were running through a thousand sparks that drifted down to the paving like fallen stars. Then there were ten thousand, maybe a hundred thousand, a red Milky Way. It was gorgeous. People by the barrier screamed and pointed at us, and I wondered why. I didn't even notice my jacket until a fireman ran over and beat it out. Except for some hair, I wasn't even singed.

On the roof of the Jack-and-Jill we stamped out embers,

directed water from a garden hose attached to the building's own outside tap, and tore up a few sections of smoldering asphalt roof. Afterward the big man — I never did learn his name — sprayed the whole roof until there were standing pools. "Oughta do it." He turned back to me. "Ya think?"

"For now. If the rest burns too long, somebody can soak it down again." I was already climbing down. "Pass the hose."

As he handed it to me, I got a good look at his eyes: tired and too full of worry. Maybe he had money in the granary. "Hell of a thing."

"Sure." I never saw him again — or, if I did, never recognized him. We were both filthy.

After that I was on hoses most of the night. One of the neighboring fire companies, from Chester, had been picnicking; they were too drunk to work their equipment. A man in unbuckled rubber boots and baggy coveralls coached me, swearing when I didn't point the hose right and weaving whether I did or not. He took three cups of coffee and stayed till two bins were almost to the ground.

That was three-thirty. My arms were aching, and my hands were full of the cold you get pumping gas without gloves in the winter. I couldn't feel my fingers on the nozzle handles. At least nobody cared when I wavered; all we were doing was keeping the fire from spreading. Guess that was all we'd ever done; a whole town had been kidding itself all night.

A man in blackface and fireman's coat stumbled up and peered along the hose. He pointed and I aimed. Suddenly he pulled the nozzle to one side. "Ah, for Jesus." He sounded like a man who'd dropped a wedding gift.

He turned and signaled. "Down. Shut 'er down, Chrissake." But he didn't much care. I shut it down. If he'd told me to tie the hose in a knot I'd have tried.

Two more regulars ran up. "Something wrong?" Nobody smiled.

"Gas leak." He pointed.

"Ah, no." But we saw it: a bright yellow flame, straight up out of nowhere, a candle in a pile of embers.

He looked from side to side, but these two were all he had. "Okay, Benny, go to Schultzie and get him to bring a jackhammer down. We'll cap it behind the pavement. Marv, scout up a couple more men and some shovels. You —" My God, he meant me. "Get the crowd moved back."

"Sure." It was easier than saying no.

"Waitaminnit. You might scare someone. Get the bullhorn off the truck." He pointed — by now his arms wavered — and I stumbled.

Bullhorn in hand, he straightened up again. There was some ex-Army in him. "Can I have your attention?" The remaining onlookers, a stiff bunch of ashen zombies, turned his way slowly. "We have a small gas leak here, so we're gonna cut off the main. There's no real danger, but we gotta clear all of you out. We'll move the barriers back half a block. You might as well go home now." He added, for no reason, "Thanks," and passed me the bullhorn.

I pushed feebly at the sawhorses with another Volunteer of the Living Dead. As we reset them I realized I'd been staring at Karl from Keller's Gas. "How do, Karl?" It was a silly thing to say, but I wasn't thinking clearly.

"Oh, fine, fine." Neither was he. "Nice of you to come help."

"Sure. I mean, uh — sure. Thanks. That the last of them?"

He looked at the bins, then realized I meant the sawhorses. "Yah, yah." He put a smile on, holding it in place by sheer will, and punched an older man's shoulder. "Come on, Pete. Might's well see if there's a place left in BeeVee to give us some beers; we ain't farmers no more."

Later I'd think about that. For now I went back to the fire. I shoveled asphalt, even ran a jackhammer till they got someone heavier, and watched as Midwest Gas capped the line. Then I went back to the hotel, found the right room in two tries, and dropped on the spare bed. Annie must have undressed me. We both had dirty jobs that night.

Chapter Eighteen

I was up the next morning by ten. That was foolish, but checkout was at eleven, so the maid (the manager's wife) did the room by noon even though I was staying. And, okay, I was nervous about Annie.

She was already dressed, packed, all but gone. I cocked an eye at the trim figure by the reading lamp. She was scanning ads, making notes in a slim black book. "You look terrific," I croaked.

"Thanks." She passed me coffee. "You look rotten. I thought private detectives always bounced back the next morning."

"If I find one like that, I'll hire him." This morning's coffee collided with last night's in my stomach. "I feel like a car bumper someone's been testing."

"Did you pass?" She put a hand on each of my cheeks and kissed my forehead and, yes, it did feel better. "Poor Nate. You taste like smoke."

"I taste smoke. Wonder if I have time to shower?" I

stood up, difficulty factor 9.3, and discovered how sore my back and arms were. "Cripes, I'm old."

"Don't say that. I'm not, and I'm barely younger than you. What's sore?"

"Most of what you see. Some of what you don't." I flexed my shoulders. Nobody was meant to hold a fire hose as long as I had. "At least I'm not the only one in town that way."

"Nate, can't you knock off for a day? Go back to bed, catch up later?"

I looked at her, and she caught it. "No, I can't join you." She slapped the paper against her leg. "I've taken too much time out of work already."

"Then don't complain about me for —"

"I know, I know. Take your shower." As I stumbled to the bathroom, she called, "By the way, nice underwear. Remember to take it off before turning on the water."

I'd have said something biting, but I was lucky she caught me.

Forty minutes later, my watch cap over my wet head, I was down at the B and V elevator, milling around and watching the locals nod to each other. You could see your breath, and most of the men had hunting caps on, the earflaps down but not tied, like Johnny Carson's farm editorials. Nobody said much.

The fire had cooled already. That should have told me something; if I'd known more about large fires, it would have. A couple of guys in black raincoats, resilient young men who looked even worse than I did, were scurrying back and forth cautiously in the ruins. From time to time a corrugated metal sheet, twisted and blackened, would shift or fall. Hardly anyone looked. The air smelled even worse than it had last night, charred and damp.

At the far end of the mess was the remaining bin, in remarkably good shape for having been through a holocaust. It was missing most of the outside metal on the near side, but other than that it was only soot-smeared and tracked with dirty streams where hoses had struck it. Maybe it wasn't a total loss. I wondered how a company dealt with leftover assets like that, how they could tell what would rot and what could be salvaged.

I wandered down that way. Two hook-and-ladder operations, clear-cut borrowings from the Twin Cities even without the decals, had pulled up. While they positioned the ladders and ran them up, looking for a solid top, some guy in the bucket of a cherry-picker was fiddling by the burned side — taking a sample, I guessed. Probably he'd bore up and down that thing all day, checking moisture levels, temperature and whatever smoke did to stored grain. Below him were a couple of portable corn dryers some hopeful had brought.

The first ladder creaked to a stop against the side wall. Wall and ladder wavered, then stabilized, and I realized that the far bin's roof was gone.

Something was bothering me. I shut my eyes. Bad goof. I wanted to lie down. After a minute I got a clear picture of last night: four bins in flames, the middle two all but gone, the one on the middle right nearly at ground level —

That was it. Even if the fire had started between bins, wouldn't it have spread evenly? I tried to remember the sparks, drifting on the wind. A hundred thousand stars — wait. They drifted every which way. Not enough wind to matter. Besides, should a fire this big have cooled this fast? Some of it was still hot, but not the part where the firemen were investigating.

I wandered over to the near hook-and-ladder and showed an older man a card I'd kept from insurance investigating. "So," I said bluntly. "What about the roof?" He gave me a hard look and shrugged. "Flash fire. Particles in suspension. Wouldn't take but a match to set it off."

I nodded, not saying, "Whose match?" There were some other suits and ties wandering around asking shrewd questions, men I knew: Hal Marino, who'd spent seven years guarding prisons and never let anyone forget it; Bert

Dreyfuss, with his empty notebook and camera memory; even Fred Durwood, who never left his office to look for anything smaller than a fifty. The rest of the detectives I didn't remember by name.

I stared up, squinting. "Which one went first?"

That got an odd look. "You don't know? Thought that was why you came down here." He jerked a thumb to one side. "This one."

"Oh, my." The one with the least damage? I tried to look tired, which wasn't hard. "Found anything?" Any money the fire was arson; even the best arsonists usually leave accidental evidence.

"Just got here."

The man in the cherry-picker shouted, "Heads up." Naturally, we ducked. Bits and pieces fluttered down nearby, and the man above growled, "There's feathers in here."

One of the suits and ties called up good-naturedly, " 'Course there is, son. Feathers make air spaces, keep the grain dry."

He scowled. "There's lots of chaff, too."

The same man called up, "In corn? You're scarin' me."

Even here that got some laughs — which set us up for the next line, as the man in the bucket leaned down and said too loudly, "Well, do they usually leave in dirt, chaff, feathers, and no corn?"

Too many people heard that. It was like one of those moments on stage where someone says, "She's my daughter," and the whole world freezes. The wise guy on the ground said, "Try ten feet over, where it's spilling." His voice was hard.

People drifted closer. A young red-headed kid scrambled up the ladder, stopping every few feet to test for stability. The hydraulics were taking most of the weight, but the whole outfit swayed more than it should have against a wall. Nobody watched him but me.

The man in the bucket called, "Dirt here. Not even more chaff."

The old fireman nodded. "Figures."

I turned to him as he waved the other ladder in place. "Why? Oh, right. Not burning."

"Chaff would go up just as fast — faster, if it was packed loose." He waved sideways; the second ladder swayed. "My guess is the top ten feet was grain, maybe more — I don't know how they take samples in these. Then, when somebody lit the top —" No more pretense. "The roof blew, lit the others. Bet they hoped this one would blow apart." He sighed. "But it didn't. And damn, there's a lot of folks gonna weep about that."

I looked at the rest of the suits and ties. They weren't weeping. Some of them wouldn't ever.

Another voice from above — this one from the first ladder. "Made it." The red-haired kid was nothing but a silhouette. "Isn't hardly warm up here." His head popped over the edge; he looked like a poster kitten, or like Charlie Chaplin on a ladder.

Then his head popped back up, and his voice was sick with fear and shock. "Oh, Jesus. Jess, get a cop. Get a cop. Oh, Lord, it's awful."

I hit the other ladder running, flashing my wallet just fast enough so no one could see anything. "Police." None of the firemen had moved.

I was ten feet up before someone called, "Who says? You sure ain't local."

I slipped, gripped tight with my hands while I got my footing. "Minneapolis. Special assignment. Check with Jon Pederson." Now it was too late to stop. Nobody could come up after me, and I couldn't back out. If I'd had time to think, I might have realized just how much trouble I was getting in. As I passed the halfway point it occurred to me that for the first time I'd used Jon's name for pull without asking him.

The wall above me swayed, and the ladder dropped a full foot. I dropped with it, not quite as fast. My hands tightened on the rungs. The people looking up seemed very small and confused. Above me and to the right the red-haired kid was still shouting how awful it was.

I took the last rung carefully. The wall clearly might topple out from under me. The wood frame at the top was charred, and the rivets were popped from the metal. If the metal pulled free while I was leaning on it, or if I leaned on the wood and it broke, I could overbalance and drop. I put a hand out cautiously. The edge was sharp, twisted by the heat.

As I poked my head over the top, I fought a crazy urge to draw my gun. Whatever it was down there, if it hadn't hurt the kid it probably wouldn't hurt me.

At first all I could see were ashes and fallen pieces of roof, thin metal beams crisscrossing. They broke everything into an untidy grid, hiding any shapes under them. I wasn't used to surveying fire damage. When my eyes adjusted to the gray and black, I tried to ignore the beams the way people peering through a fence ignore the links.

That made it easy to recognize the hand, black and splay-fingered where it rose, curled toward the sky like a dead spider's legs. The metal band that had bound his wrist to the beam shone where spray from a hose had cleaned it. You could see how far it had burned into the arm.

Now that I knew what to look for, it was easy to find the other hand, the arms, the twisted body. You could even make out what was left of the face and the eye sockets. The kid was right; it was awful.

Whoever had crucified him on a crossbeam had figured the fire would hide the evidence. In one of the normal bins that would have been true; this one simply never got hot enough. I leaned forward for a final look, putting more weight on the wall.

No matter what Bernie says, I'm not overweight. I am heavy enough so that when the wall I leaned on dropped a foot, my weight drove the sharp edge into my left hand.

I clutched tight, even with the cut hand. Somewhere below, I heard cries and wondered if they were for me. I edged to the right, where a charred crossbeam still hung in place high enough to get me back in balance. My feet were still on the ladder. My cut hand left damp patches on the blackened edge.

It was very quiet below, except for the guy in the cherry-picker: "What's goin' on? Something wrong?" I wished someone would shut him up.

The red-haired kid, a pro in spite of shock, called across the bin, "Hold still. I'll shift over —" I shook my head as gently as I could. This wall was swaying when I moved now; by the time they moved the ladder I'd be long gone.

It couldn't have been more than a minute or two before the beam was above my hand. I could see the charred hole the holding-bolts had burned for themselves. No wonder the metal was loose. If I reached up and the beam held I was home free —

If I did that I'd put all my weight on one hand, on the metal. Either I reached for life with my cut hand, or I pushed off it and widened the cut while I shoved the wall down.

I forgot about Colfax and the gun in the bin, and I hadn't been thinking about Roy lately anyway. Part of me felt sad that the last thing I focused on, desperately and intent, was a charred piece of rough pine.

Now.

I whipped my good hand up, trying not to feel as I shoved my left down onto a jagged edge. My right slid over the beam . . . slipped on ashes . . . groped . . . caught.

The metal dropped out from under my hand, scoring the cut on its way by. My palm, in two parts, felt unnatural. Later it would start hurting again.

I put my left hand on the beam, readjusted my feet on

the ladder, arched my back as the corrugated-metal sheet fell completely away. Then I exhaled and took a last look over the edge at what I was sure had to be Frees's body. My second talk with him and the failed attempt on his life must have panicked someone.

By that time it's amazing I could notice anything, but the sun must have caught the corpse's gold teeth perfectly, to make them shine in all that ash. I'd seen those teeth once before, by night, in a mouth slack-jawed with shock and grief.

I didn't quite fall off the ladder at the bottom; someone caught me. Then there was a cloth wrapped around my hand, and someone said, firmly but reassuringly, "Easy, fella." I looked into the face of the older man, who looked worried for me and mad at me at the same time. That made him the fire chief. "You're lucky," he said without anger.

I nodded, then turned my head toward the crowd. "Anybody seen Emil Firebourne this morning?"

They looked around blankly. I winced as my hand kicked in; the pain was back. My God, it was back. "I think I have. Call Farrell."

After that I lay back down. Annie had her wish; I was taking some time off.

Chapter Nineteen

Neither Annie nor I said much on the way to the car. She was "yupping," answering like angry people sometimes do. I wasn't surprised.

As we left Belle View I said, "Thanks for coming down. I would've been happy to take the bus."

"No problem." So much for starting conversation.

I looked out the window. In an hour or two it would be dark; the days were getting shorter. Finally I said, "Did you take the bus?"

She braked abruptly for a tractor. "I hitched."

"You're kidding."

"A friend dropped me at 35. A trucker took me to 63. Guy who works in a creamery west of here drove me into town." She didn't look at me.

"Annie, you're a grown-up, but hitching is crazy. You could get hurt —"

Now she turned, her lips pressed to nothing and her eyes hard. "Well, that's just a damn shame, Nate. Especially when everybody I know is so damn careful all the time."

She swerved back into her own lane. Even in my own car, I didn't want to speak to her about that just now.

After a while she said, "How's your hand?"

"Hurts." I held it up and stared. Swathed in gauze with a brace on it, it barely looked or felt like part of me. The doctor said if I took care of it I'd get full use of the fingers back. I'd always have the scar.

"Did he give you anything for it?"

"Painkillers. I won't need them till the novocaine wears off. They're strong stuff — no drinking, driving or charades when I take them." Except for sleeping, I wouldn't take them.

"Did he tell you to get some rest?"

"He said, 'Get as much rest as you can.' I'll try." I shifted in the seat, holding my left hand steady with my right. "I'll have to figure out how I'm getting back down here —"

"God damnit, Nate." There were tears in her eyes. I hadn't expected that; maybe I'm stupid. "Leave it alone. Go back to work, make bunches of money, go to Bermuda with me this winter and forget the whole damn thing." She added, half to the steering wheel, "I'm sorry I ever told you."

"Even if I thought I should quit now, I can't. Whoever did that last bit with Emil — watch the road."

"I'm watching."

"Okay, sorry. Annie, this isn't like a building going up. If a contracter quits, you yell at him or you sue him, but you find somebody else to finish. Or if you're rich and crazy, you just let it stay half finished. Because when somebody quits a building, nobody gets killed."

"Nobody'd follow you to the Twin Cities." But she didn't say it with much conviction.

I said as gently as I could, "That's where this started."

We rode on, and there wasn't another sound but the windshield wipers. If the rain had come twenty-four hours earlier, life might be a lot different just now. I knew she liked me, but I didn't understand why she was so upset.

Annie slowed down. "What is this?"

"Farm auction." There were pickups, both sides of the road, and the family mailbox taken down already. That shot the rest of the day.

Annie slowed way down; there wasn't much room for through traffic. I said, "Ever seen one of these?"

"I'm a city girl, remember?" She peered into the farmyard. "It's all grown-ups. Aren't these family farms in here?"

"Sure, but nobody takes the kids to these. It's like shielding them from car accidents or bloody news footage." There were middle-aged men in hunting caps with the flaps down, and young men in earmuffs and a battered couple who might have been refugees but were probably the family who was selling.

"Which ones are the owners?"

I gestured to the refugees. "Those two. That guy with the stetson is the auctioneer, any money." The only man who didn't hunch over and pull his collar tighter when he looked toward the house. Auctioneers have feelings, too, but they're used to it. They hold the owner together, do their job and leave. They may say something kind later, but for now they have to be hard.

"I bet there's some rough bargaining going on there."

I said, "I doubt it. You don't lie to jack prices at a farm auction. These are your neighbors, and you've got to look them in the eye later and say, 'You knew what you was buying.' So you show the welds and the dents, and you tell how the motor kicks in so hard the body rattles over the frame, and they buy it anyway. Suddenly you're holding a check or a wad of money you owe the bank, and it's all gone."

Annie shivered. "That's awful. There's really nothing else they can do?"

"You do everything else first. Sometimes —" I waved my bad hand and winced. The feeling was starting to come back into it. "Sometimes nothing else works. People get trapped. After they give up and admit it, they start feeling trapped. After that, you'd be surprised at the crazy things they do, just from fear."

Annie peered at the wet asphalt, trying to sound casual. "You've known from the beginning that I could identify them for you."

I didn't have to ask. "I've known you could try. You saw two middle-aged men once, in a bar, months ago."

"I still know." She added, "Emil wasn't one of them."

"He wouldn't be; he — oh, God. You went and looked, at Emil didn't you? Pictures, or the body?" I thought of that body and thought of something else, quickly.

"Both. Nate, I could do it. When am I going to?"

"When you do it through one-way glass at a city police station."

"Couldn't you use my I.D. for the arrest?"

"Sure — and they'd get out if we — if I didn't get anything more solid. And you'd be looking over your shoulder the rest of your life, checking your car for bombs, waiting for your apartment to catch fire."

"Nice to know you're so worried." But her voice sounded strange. "I'll keep out of things. Listen, I have a plan."

"For what?" Just now I'd accept any ideas at all. I shut my eyes. There was no way Annie could have viewed that body without explaining why she wanted to. I hoped, silently, that I was wrong to suspect Sheriff Josh Farrell of anything.

"For supper. We're going to the top of the Kahler in Rochester."

"That's fifty miles out of our — oh."

"Not from here. Some two-lane blacktops and we're there. That's why I took country roads north."

Good point. "I wasn't paying attention. Okay; whose turn is it to pay?"

"Mine."

"No argument. How's the food?"

"Cosmic, but wait'll you see the view." She whipped sideways and sped up. Belle View was already far behind us.

She was right about the view. We stared out at the sunset; Annie pointed to one of the older Mayo buildings, covered with concrete squirrels and acorns in a geometric style she called Art Deco. I stared further, to the city park. The Zumbro River runs through it. Nearby there's a pond that stays unfrozen all winter. Couple that with a healthy population of breadcrumb-toting citizens and you have some fine reasons for geese not to migrate.

The geese know the reasons, but they're restless. Every day they form a wedge, fly north, fly south, and settle back down on the pond and the Zumbro. Even asleep they're restless. A wing flaps, somebody hisses, and pretty soon the whole bunch is in the air again: north, south, home. The food's good enough, and the water's clear, but something's wrong.

What bothered me this fall was like that. It would be nice if it were something in the air, like the wild geese around Rochester, but it's not. It's more mundane, more painful. Your father's worst enemy dies, and your father's best friend dies, and one day no better than either of those your father dies. It's that first deadly frost, no longer in the air, but settled.

One morning you wake up and see the rime of white on your head, hardly enough to notice, and you don't feel any different, but you're dying. Give it fifty years. And for the first time you know how long fifty years is. And it might not be that long: you might make it to eighty or more, but when it comes to death, it's open season. That hurts.

And if my dad could hear me thinking that, he'd snort. "You hurt? I *died*."

Right, Dad. I almost forgot.

Finally I said, "Annie?"

"Still here." And I realized that it was dark, the meal had come, and I'd said next to nothing.

"You don't like Marlowe much, do you?"

She looked startled; I guess she'd expected something else. "Not much. He's okay. I like cats well enough. Look, do I have to? I don't think he likes me."

"No, no. Sometimes I don't like him much, either. He's a thug." I finished my drink — my wine. When did that come? I was crashing.

"It's just — you know I let him out when I'm away? I figure he can't trash the place if he's outside." I paused. "I leave food on the back porch. Sometimes I leave two or three days' worth, in case I'm away longer than I planned."

She nodded.

"What I'm asking is, the next time I go to Belle View could you stop and check on him? You don't need to talk to him or anything —" I realized I was babbling, but I couldn't stop. "Just call him and see if he comes. It's crazy, but lately I've been worried. He's older now, but he still gets into fights —"

I couldn't pick up my glass while she held my hand, but that didn't bother me. "And it's so dangerous out there. I just hate to think of him lying somewhere hurt, or in pain, or —"

"He'll be fine."

"Maybe." I swallowed. "I dunno why I'm doing this. He's pretty tough."

"Sure he is." She squeezed my hand and smiled into my eyes. "I've noticed something."

"What's that?" Nathan Phillips, all-purpose straight man.

"You've never told me you're tough. You tell everybody how tough your cat is. I think that's how you make up for not saying how tough you are." The smile faded. "And this time you're telling me Marlowe isn't tough enough."

"He's fine." I was surprised at how angry I sounded.

Annie laughed and said in my own sharp farm-town voice, " 'Nobody's as tough as my damn cat.' Okay, he's tough. You're not. You've said so, right? Or you've never said you were. Tell me what you're scared of."

So I did. I told her how Colfax and Ada Firebourne each died, and how Frees and little Kathy nearly got killed, and I asked her what kind of maniac thought up Emil's death, and I said how it felt to hang forty or fifty feet up from a bleeding hand. And suddenly I was telling her about the bomb in my car and how frightened I'd been for her, and how it really had been for her, even though I'd been pretty worried for myself. I wanted to say more, but we were getting off the subject.

She pulled her hair back over her shoulders, an oddly young gesture. "I can take care of myself."

"Not if you don't know what I'm getting you into."

"I'll risk it."

"I don't want you hurt."

"Nate, you could say that about anything, not just detective work. People take risks. They get hurt. Sometimes they think it's worth it."

The coffee had come. Maybe that was what made me a little brighter for once. "Know what? I think you talk about danger and risk the way I talk about Marlowe. To say something else, I mean."

"I don't get it." So I dropped it. Maybe it wasn't a good time.

The drive back to Minneapolis was quiet, but this time it was a good-natured silence. We stopped at my place — I made her wait in the car until I'd checked it — and fed Marlowe. He rubbed against her, which I thought was a terrific sign until I remembered she'd had the flounder at dinner. We should have asked for a kitty bag. We threw him back out and went to her place, where it was safe. Afterward I tried to stay awake, brooding about dragging Annie into danger even if it was her choice, but I was too tired; hand and all, I dropped off pretty quickly.

Chapter Twenty

Arlis Schmidt was in the front yard, doubled over a rake. She had on a jacket and shawl, and her ankles were swathed in Ace bandages.

She waved an arm. "Such a mess this morning," she said embarrassedly. "Not fit to be seen."

I nearly said something about her clothes, then realized she meant the yard. "It's fine. I wondered when you worked on this yard; it's always so tidy."

"Oh, now." She seemed about to call me "fresh." "It looks terrible this morning, I'm sure."

"It's lovely." And it was; the light ground fog was dissipating, and all the trees around were silhouetted against it like cutouts as the sun burned through. "If you don't mind my asking, how are your legs this morning?"

"A little sore. I've been out in the damp too much." She added with completely uncoquettish frankness, "My ankles swell, if I don't watch it. Once I could dance all night and walk two miles home to start cleaning. Now four or five hours in the yard lay me low." She glanced at my hand. "You have some bandages, too."

I lifted my swathed left hand. "Souvenir of the fire. I guess you heard about it."

She nodded, pleased. "Next day. You ought to be more careful, Mr. Phillips. I'll bet you upset that young woman who came down to see you." She nodded again to herself. "She got angry."

I gaped. "Were you in the car with us, and I didn't notice?"

She ducked her head, smiling. "Oh, now. It just figures, that's all." Then she looked me straight in the eye. "I hear you did a good job at that fire."

"Thanks. So did everyone else. Didn't help much, did it?"

"Of course not. When these things start, they move to their finish. People can't stop them any more than they can stop a blizzard." I wondered if she were speaking of something else besides the fire. "Would you like to come in? I have coffee on, and there's some toast and jam."

"I'd enjoy that."

Inside, the damp was less chilling; old people often keep their houses hot, and Arlis Schmidt was no exception. This time I noticed how many of her house plants were succulents and cacti: burro's tail, Christmas cactus, mother-in-law tongue, and some others I didn't recognize.

She insisted on carrying the tray herself. "Please move my reading," she said anxiously, and I scrambled to pick WHAT IF YOU DIED RIGHT NOW? and NUCLEAR WAR: IS IT ARMAGEDDON? off the coffee table. She put a lot of artificial energy into things this morning. "Now," and she sounded falsely bright, "how is your investigation?"

"Awful." She'd know if I was lying. "You know about Emil. Also, someone tried to kill me. Someone tried to kill Brian Frees, and nearly killed a little girl by mistake."

The brightness disappeared, and her eyes got sharp. "Dora Mahler's child, or Nancy's?"

"I wouldn't know, ma'am. Uh, Frees's niece, Kathy."

"Dora's." She settled back, holding her cup tightly. "Poor Dora. That pretty child was a terrible birth, and so weak and pale they didn't think she'd live — even with the wonders they do in hospitals these days. She's a treasure to Dora. It was at Brian Frees's place, was it?" I nodded. "Dora hates to leave her with a regular sitter, she's that afraid for that child."

"She wasn't harmed."

Arlis leaned forward. "Tell me about it," she said, and I've seldom heard such hunger.

When I finished she sat back and sighed. "I won't tell anyone about that. Dora would hear, and it would flutter her heart for years. Kathy won't tell her; thank the dear Lord I'll be gone by the time that child's a teenager. Do you know who did it?"

"No."

She shrugged, then grabbed at her sliding shawl. She hadn't taken anything off when she came in, hot as the house was. "That's a shame. Some things just stay secret, I s'pose."

"I have to keep looking." I set my coffee down and added less firmly, "Mrs. Schmidt, what if I stopped?"

"What if you did?" She set her own cup down and pointed out the window. "There's a hundred and more houses that way. Which of them would weep that you left, that nothing happened, that things went on as they are? Things go on, you know. You and I can't stop them or turn them. What God wants for us, God gets, and all the pushing and tugging in the world can't turn or stop it."

I could have said something polite, could have ignored her advice and made her happy. It wouldn't have been right; she was someone to take seriously, not some scared kid.

I thought, then answered carefully. "Mrs. Schmidt, once I could have done that. It would have been easy, if I'd only thought of it, to put it all in the back of my mind and never come here. Now I can't do that. I don't think it would change things if I stopped, unless it changed them for the worse."

She motioned with a stiff right hand for me to go on. I swallowed. "Someone from the state's going to look into that granary. It was the world's easiest embezzlement — keep the books straight, but steal the product and charge storage on it. I still don't know how they passed inspections."

"It'll come out." She sounded tired, worn.

"At least one, probably two of the shareholders in the B and V will go to jail. There had to be a local involved; Danny Lowenbach hasn't lived here long enough to know which truckers would keep quiet about shipments and how to find buyers that wouldn't gossip to local farmers. But if I leave now, Danny will ask the questions. Once he has some hard evidence, he'll ask till he finds out which one did it. And Mrs. Schmidt, Danny won't give up at all. He's had his horse shot out from under him one time too many; this granary and the businesses with it were his last chance. Do you think he'll drop it?"

She shook her head, a small motion over a stiffly held body.

"Like I said, things will happen fast. The man that killed my partner, that tried to kill me and Frees and that killed Ada and Emil Firebourne won't sit and wait for Danny. I think we've both figured out that the man who thought those deaths up isn't anywhere near sane."

She opened her mouth, then shut it tight. Right then I would have given a lot to hear what she had to say, but after waiting I went on.

"If I left now, someday someone still might come to kill me. He might succeed, even though I'm more of a pro than I used to admit. But here in Belle View he'll be sure to move fast, and he'll have a free shot at any number of people that aren't ready."

She looked at me sharply. "Innocent people?"

I thought. "Not quite."

She nodded. "I thought you'd see that. And you?"

I wasn't sure what she meant. "I'm not going to kill anybody, but I'm not innocent either." It felt strange saying that; everyone feels younger than he is. "But guilty people stand too close to people like Kathy Mahler, and I stand too near people that . . . matter to me."

I set down my cup, spreading my hands. "Somewhere along the line, I made things like this my job. Maybe I will hurt somebody, but leaving things to happen on their own would be like watching a house on fire and not telling anyone."

"Not like starting it," she said gently.

"Right." And it felt better that way, knowing I hadn't started things. I wasn't hell raising or starting quarrels. I hadn't called Roy to start this, or killed him. "It's like the granary fire; if it isn't stopped, who knows who it could hurt?" I stopped. The granary fire was out, but it was still hurting plenty of people in Gordon County. "Do you se why I have to keep going?"

She said softly, almost sullenly, "Get some paper." I took my notebook out. "No. You'll need more than that. In the writing desk in the hall."

I rummaged through it and found five sheets and a mechanical pencil from a homeowners' insurance company. "Will these do?"

"Fine." She had her eyes closed.

"Are you all right?"

She opened one eye. "Sit." I sat. "Listen carefully —"

For the next hour I took more notes than I had in my whole first term at the U. of Minnesota.

"These are the things you wouldn't find out in time. Some of them won't make sense unless you know a lot more than I do. Maybe they'll help some." She didn't sound like she believed that. "You've talked to Brian Frees."

"As much as he would."

"And Emil Firebourne?"

"Nope." And damn Farrell for steering me away. And myself for letting him.

"Anyone else?"

"Niles Swenson. I know he's land-poor, and I know about some of his debts."

"And you know he shot at Danny Lowenbach and Sammy Detweiler."

"Ye — wait. Sammy?" That round, worried little realtor that I'd seen in Emil's barn?

"Josh Farrell doesn't know about this. Niles had a temper, you know." She stared toward the front door. "Back when he was in high school, I can remember running out that door and pulling Niles off one of the Ptacek brothers before he beat him to death. The Ptacek boy had called him a big, dumb Swede sodbuster." She turned to me and smiled. "Doesn't sound like much, does it? But Niles's grandparents *were* sodbusters — homesteaders, with no money. Fifteen years after that fistfight, the Ptacek farm went up for sale and Niles bought it, then resold it. I think he just wanted it for a month."

"About Sammy —"

"I haven't forgotten. I wanted to explain how Niles feels about his land. Well, after the recession, maybe two years back, or three, Sammy went out to try to talk Niles into selling thirty or forty acres. Sammy had some foolish scheme; he always does — a storage place for those big rolling irrigation outfits you see nowadays, or a feed lot — and he thought Niles had the best location. He said he'd heard Niles was pressed for money and he'd be willing to take some land off Niles's hands for a good price."

I winced. Arlis caught me, and nodded approvingly.

"Niles had a second gun that Josh hadn't taken. Niles chased Sammy down that long lane with it, and shot over his head once. Sammy walked into town, didn't want anyone to know. Niles parked Sammy's car in front of the

Lutheran church after the service, with a note pinned to it."

"And Sammy wouldn't forget that."

"He couldn't. He ended up buying a worse patch of land for more money. Probably he thinks that's why he went under that time. I imagine he and his realty office — he owns it with the Mishak boy — are still paying for that."

"But would Sammy ruin himself to get Niles?"

"No. Niles would ruin himself to ruin Sammy. But Sammy may not have a chance of making it and might not worry too much about taking Niles with him. For that matter," she looked at me over her glasses, "I don't know much about business, but I do know that all partners aren't equal. Couldn't Sammy ruin Niles and still be safe?"

"True." I wondered how I could bully Danny into letting me see the partnership agreement. "So you think Sammy needed the money."

"Not as badly as some. Kevin Riley, that man who owns Riley Rambler — have you spoken to him?" I'd seen his face, his building, his flashy car. "He owns almost the whole block his dealership is on. He bought it when times were better for American cars. Now he has all kinds of mortgages and loans, and I don't for the life of me see how he's surviving, if the quiet in his showroom is any sign. If he doesn't do something, he'll be a bankrupt soon." She sounded disapproving. Even to someone who had lived through the Thirties, bankruptcy wasn't respectable.

I kept writing. "The domestic car market's taken a beating. At least the gas stations are doing all right."

"Ah. That's the sad part."

"That the gas stations are doing all right?"

"No, that Virgil Keller sold the Sunrise Oil company and invested. Every last penny that didn't go to running the station or putting Warren and Willy through college went into the B and V Elevator — and you can't tell me that Virgil knew enough to protect himself from those people, from Niles and Sammy and Ed Parker and that Danny Lowenbach." She shook her head. "No one I know has talked to Virgil since the fire. I'm afraid for that man."

"You mentioned Ed Parker."

"Parker Drugs. It used to have a soda stand, and it was about half the size it is now. Now it's Rainey's, of course; Ed Parker sold the business but kept the building. His father founded that business," she said, tight-lipped. Selling was almost as bad as going bankrupt. "That family's been in the country club here for three generations, since it opened. Bobby Parker was on the golf team, and I hear he's on it at Yale now. Oh, yes, there's a Belle View boy at Yale," she said with pride. "He was talking about becoming a doctor and coming back. We'll have to see what happens to his tuition."

Arlis had an uncomfortable way of making money less abstract. "But what did Ed Parker put his money into?"

"Practically anything Danny Lowenbach told him to. This is his third time investing with that Danny Lowenbach, and at least this one was working out." Then she said the only sympathetic thing she ever directed toward Danny. "The one time Danny gets a business going and stays with it, and one of his own partners destroys it. Poor man, I wonder where he'll go."

"This is his home now," I put in.

Arlis looked startled at that. "Oh, no. He's from Illinois." I guess you do stay an out-of-towner for a long time.

She told me about Pat Cavanaugh, how when he'd become a lawyer in his father's firm he'd planned to be the richest man in the county and had more unrented land to show for it than anyone else. She told me other things, too: more details about Ada's and Emil's marriage, and Emil's investments in corn futures. Everyone said they had paid off, but you had to wonder. That had been some time back, three years, maybe.

I sat up. "Two years, maybe?"

She blinked. "Why, yes. That's right, because it was the spring that Vera Ronald walked out on the Gordon boy, and her in her dressing gown leaving a Main Street apartment. How did you guess?"

"Just lucky." He had paid his debts, and he could afford to blow the whistle on the B and V Elevator Company. But one of his partners had murdered Roy — for next to nothing, I realized bitterly — and Emil had kept his mouth shut, probably reinvested, and hadn't even needed a second warning until Ada finally blew up. That was when someone had killed Ada, partly to silence her and partly to silence Emil without any chance of his estate liquidating the granary investment. And in the end it hadn't hidden a thing. My God: Roy, Ada, all of them, had been killed for nothing.

"Are you listening, Mr. Phillips?"

"Yes'm." And listen I did. She told me about each investor: his marriage, his children, the family he'd lost and the money he'd made, and vice versa. At the end of it I had five pages scribbled on both sides and a far sharper idea of what questions to ask from here. I hoped I'd have the chance to ask them.

I stood up. "Thank you so much, Mrs Schmidt. I'll try and use this —" I paused. What could I say? "I'll try to finish this with as little harm as possible."

"Finish, then." She had picked up a pamphlet and was clutching it as though she could draw strength from it. "Do what you must and try not to get hurt."

There wasn't much to say to that. "I'm sure what you've told me will help." I walked to the door, then turned around. "One thing: didn't anyone in town suspect that the granary was in trouble?"

She turned her head to the right, staring out her window toward downtown. "Until the other night," she said slowly, "the B and V Elevator Company looked like the soundest business in town."

She laughed, a dry sound with a lot of sadness in it. "You want to know something? It still does."

That took me a second. I nodded and left. The wind had picked up outside, and the day looked grayer than I'd expected. Fall would end quickly this year, and winter would be hard.

Chapter Twenty-One

I was downtown before nine-thirty, which I thought was pretty good considering how little I was sleeping these days. At least I'd had coffee this time. I considered taking a Percodan to ease the pain in my left hand, but decided against it.

The shop fronts were just as quiet, just as secret as the first time. Maybe it was my imagination, but there seemed to be even fewer people on the streets. Roy used to love having the morning all to himself; here I could understand that. Me, I'm normally comfortable with crowds.

Once you're used to a city, the early-morning quiet of a small town is beyond belief. The only noises I heard were a truck backfiring on a side street and a stone I must have kicked skittering near my feet. I was headed toward the Crystal Café in the middle of the block, glancing casually at the merchandise dimly visible in security-lit stores.

This time when the truck backfired I realized I hadn't heard any motor noise. This time when the stone skittered, I saw it chip out of the brick next to me.

I flattened into the doorway of the five-and-dime shop, hand inside my coat. I couldn't bring myself to draw my gun; it seemed too unreal. No one else had run outside; no one had called out or noticed. A block and a half away a woman with a stroller pushed across Main Street, jaywalking. Here that usually wasn't dangerous. I opened my mouth to shout to her, then shut it as a web of cracks appeared in the glass door behind and above me. The woman finished crossing the street and turned away from me, rolling on.

Nobody was near me. Nobody was visible, on the sidewalk or the roof or in windows. The five-and-dime wasn't open. I pounded on an uncracked side window; nobody came to help me. Another bullet scored the concrete behind me and whined off. Apparently, nobody heard that, either.

I considered battering my way through the door, but gave up. That would mean turning my back squarely to the street. It also might mean cutting my other hand up; then I'd be helpless. I hesitated, then dashed forward and sideways, heading for the next doorway.

Whistle-Stop Clothiers was good to me. The gunman, rattled by my motion, shot a nasty chip out of the mannequin in the window. If it was intentional it wasn't a bad shot. I still couldn't see anybody. The street was empty and peaceful, and this couldn't be happening.

I leaned from the entryway, looking sideways. When you're eighty or have emphysema you know how long a city block can be. Otherwise, it takes something special to remind you. This block stretched a heartbreaking distance in either direction. The left corner was marginally closer.

I pounded on the door of the clothing shop. If anyone was inside, they didn't care to come to the door. Maybe this was execution by consent; I was no longer welcome in Belle View.

I looked toward the Crystal Café. Suddenly I didn't

need coffee to stay awake. If I could kick the door open, I could leap inside and roll out of the line of fire.

On the other hand, if my sniper had help, what better place to pin me down? I pictured myself rolling in, coming up to my knees, facing a gun from the booths. Nasty thought.

I shook my head. Why would anyone bother with sniping if they could pick me off inside? I pulled my gun out and watched the cornices across the street. At least I had one advantage; I was looking north and west, and whoever was shooting at me might get some sun in his eyes. I scanned along the street, past Kruger's Bakery, past the furniture store, past the Corner Jeweler.

I caught the glint of a rifle barrel above the bakery. I rolled, pulled my gun, took aim.

The door of Whistle-Stop Clothiers shattered where I'd been standing. Cheap glass, I guess. An alarm went off.

So did my gun. I felt silly, firing a snub-nose thirty-eight at a target across the street; it felt a lot like that poster of the trapped rat making an obscene gesture at a stooping eagle: "The last act of defiance."

It worked, though: the rifle barrel pulled back hastily, and I sprinted for the corner faster than I'd ever run in high school. Around the corner I hugged the building, panting. After a few seconds I noticed that I'd hit my left hand rounding the corner. Maybe I'd take that Percodan after all.

My car was behind the hotel, on the other side of Main Street. I jogged two blocks south and three blocks over, and crossed over between Riley Rambler and a gas station. I ran up an alley until I was even with the courthouse and crossed sideways two blocks to the sheriff's office. I still hadn't seen a living soul, not even a school child. Was someone keeping them off the streets? It was a great morning for paranoia.

I looked both ways, then ran into the sheriff's office,

straight past the dispatcher's desk. "Sheriff —" I stopped.

Daisy barked. "Quiet, Daisy." Farrell looked up from polishing and cleaning his rifle. There was a half-empty ammunition box on the desk. His eyes were noncommittal. "Yessir?"

"Nothing." I spun around and left. Turning my back on him was the hardest thing I'd done in a long time.

Chapter Twenty-Two

I entered the café through the back door. I wasn't ready for Main Street again. Small-town restaurants let you do things like that; the Crystal Café had a hand-painted sign over its back door, facing the parking lot.

I almost hadn't come at all; a half-hour of thinking had calmed me down, but hadn't made me reckless. On the other hand, if I was staying in Belle View at all, there were a couple questions I'd better ask at the café.

Tom and Gertie saw me before I was halfway up the aisle. Gertie scowled; Tom merely looked nervous and waved a hand out of the booth. I didn't have to guess who they'd be sitting with.

The cracks in the front door had tape stretched hastily across them, and a sign scrawled on white wrapping paper said, "CAREFUL: BROKEN GLASS." I nodded at Cora, who had stopped cleaning the counter to stare at me. "Looks like you've had some excitement."

She wasn't glad to see me, either. "Kids broke it." Maybe she believed that.

I pulled a chair over. "Tom, Gertie, Homer." I said. "Pretty quiet today."

Gertie snorted. Tom nodded quickly, Homer a minute later.

"It's that granary," Gertie said, clattering her spoon. "You can't spend what you don't have."

"Maybe that's it." Maybe I should quit thinking of Dodge City. People weren't that nervous, except for me.

And except for Homer. He was facing the bullet hole, and he was clearly spooked by it. "Some of it's busier than it looks." He smiled sickly.

Cora brought coffee. I needed it, now. "Still, won't the fire be covered? Insurance —"

"Can't insure dirt." Tom sounded angry and vicious. "Insurance company's saying they can't be sure it wasn't just chaff in the other bins. Not that I blame 'em. Somebody sold this county a bill of goods."

I looked at him, surprised. Where had all this energy — this anger — come from? He seemed three inches taller and full of a strength I'd never seen when he'd been cowed by Gertie.

Gertie said, "We'll do fine, Tom." She laid a hand on his arm, then moved it back across the table where I hadn't noticed it before — holding Homer's left hand.

Homer said listlessly, "Sure. We'll get some money on the dollar. None of us needs that much." He smiled again, barely. "Maybe now we can talk ourselves into moving in together."

I must be blind. I know I come close, particularly where romance is concerned. I turned to Tom. "Did you have anything in it?"

He shrugged. "My money's in Huffman's Bank. I guess it'll be okay." Tears came into his eyes. "God, Homer, whatever you two need —"

"I know. Thanks, Tom."

"God, if there was just something a man could do —"

Homer said calmly, "There isn't, any more. Guess there never was," and I knew.

I finished my coffee, then said easily. "Quite a shot through that window. Care to give it a quick look, Homer?"

He nodded, setting down his cup. I stood back behind him while he got out, then took his right arm to walk him to the front. Tom called after me, "He's plenty strong."

Gertie shushed him. "He doesn't mean any harm." I hadn't, not to Homer or to anyone else.

At the door we looked studiously at the cracks. Homer said quietly, "You can let go now."

"Right." I stood partway behind him, slipping the gun from his pocket into mine. "A twenty-two. Pretty lightweight. Target pistol?" He nodded. "Not your gun?"

He shook his head. "I own a forty-five. Army. But it's too heavy now."

"Who gave you the twenty-two?" He didn't answer. "Okay. Later, I guess. But it was your rifle, right? That's how you knew you needed a lighter gun."

"I tried." He was apologizing for missing. "Rested it on the brickwork, and still it was too heavy. Used to be I could carry that thing for miles —"

"Just like Niles Swenson. Ever hunt with him? You know, I thought you were him, this morning."

"Niles wouldn't miss." He was proud of Niles, ashamed of unsuccessful sniping.

"Yeah, that's what I figured. You wouldn't believe who else I thought you were. You were the car bomb, too, weren't you?"

This time I held his arm to steady him. "That should have worked. It would have worked. I still can't see what saved you."

"Careful habits." Mostly luck.

"How did you figure it out?"

"You mean who did it? The bomb was too nice, too

delicate for a car bomb. Bombs aren't usually subtle; you made a jeweler's weapon. Repaired a lot of watches, didn't you?'' I decided against telling him there were easier ways to blow someone up. ''Keller or Riley supplied the parts. For a while I thought one of them did it, but they didn't know as much about me as you did. Homer, why?''

''Money.'' A glance back toward the table. ''Other reasons. I thought I could stop you in time —''

''Not this time, though. Was this revenge for my ruining the granary?'' He shut his eyes and nodded. ''You really think that, don't you? But I didn't do a thing to the B and V. I didn't light fires, and I didn't steal from it. The man that talked you into shooting at me is the one that ruined you, Homer. Who was he?''

''I don't have to say.'' But his voice trembled.

''You can't say. Because it's only about a tenth revenge; the rest is a last crazy try at keeping out of bankruptcy, maybe out of jail for fraud. You couldn't help the man who bought your store after you retired. That means whatever you got for the sale of the store went somewhere. Into a partnership, maybe?''

He didn't say anything. I went on, ''And you still have a partner who runs your money, and he's got you where he wants you. Homer, you're no avenging angel; you're an errand boy in debt to a psychotic. For the last time, who is he?''

''I won't say.''

''Not to me. But if I were you I'd turn state's evidence, now. Because it's over. Even though one crazy man out there — you know his name — won't admit it. And God knows who he'll kill if you don't walk into Farrell's office and say who he is.''

That turned his head. ''You're not taking me there?''

''Nope.'' I felt too sick. I'd liked Homer, and I'd liked this town when I first saw it. ''If you go in yourself, you might cut a deal. If I take you in, you draw jail time. Even a little —''

"A little is all I have." His voice gained strength momentarily, out of fear. "Gertie . . ."

"Didn't have a thing to do with it." Gertie, who was strong enough to lift a car hood. Gertie, who could open the roof trap and pass up a rifle.

Homer nodded. "Right."

He wanted to say something else, but I cut him off. I had something I needed him to say. "The money people from the granary are all hidden somewhere. You know where?"

"I think so."

I glanced back at the table. Tom and Gertie were getting restless. "We'll have to get back to the booth."

"How did you know Gertie didn't have a gun?" He added hastily, "Or Tom?"

"The one with the gun would face the front door; out-of-towners never come in the back way. Um, I kind of hoped you wouldn't shoot me in front of witnesses anyway."

"I don't know if I could have."

"Homer, who gave you the gun? Who talked you into sniping at me, bombing my car? He's still out there, and he's bound to kill someone else."

I held my breath and waited. Finally he said, "They're out at Emil's hunting lodge off the Zumbro River. Have to be. That's where they always went to talk." He added wistfully, "I used to hunt out there, but I never got invited to meetings."

"Thanks." I let go of his arm. "But you won't tell me which one it is. Protecting a friend? An old friend?"

"I have to sit down. My legs are tired." I wasn't surprised. He'd had a very active morning.

"Sure. Homer? Talk to the sheriff. If you won't tell me, that name is a hole card. Use it. It could keep you and" — I stumbled — "other people . . . out of trouble."

As I pulled the door open gingerly, he asked, "You're going out there?"

"Sure. Why not? Think about what I said." I walked

away. What else can you say to a man who tried to kill you?

I wondered what he'd tell Gertie, and whether she'd let him talk. It wasn't my problem. Homer and I both had too much to think about.

Josh Farrell was cleaning his desk. He wasn't the Pederson type; it stayed messy after he got done. "Dunno why I even try. Chances are what you bring in'll mess me up even more."

"This time I'm tidying up." I took a deep breath and popped the pistol onto his desk. "Check that for two sets of prints. One set, if I didn't foul them up, will be from the man who set everything up."

He tried to put a pencil up the barrel, like people do in the movies. My turn to grin. "Unless you have a twenty-two pencil, that's not gonna work."

He scowled. "Has it been fired?"

"Not today, that I know of." Then I caught what he meant. "Sure. If it wasn't used since it changed hands, then the last print on the trigger —"

"Might be the gun owner's. If it ain't smeared." He nudged it into a plastic bag and put it in a drawer. "We may send it to your buddies in Minneapolis; we're not too good with fingerprinting here, if you recall from that car bomb." He waited for my reaction. "I just gave you a chance to smart-mouth me. What you waiting for?"

I only said, "I thought you were better at fingerprinting than you let on."

It took a second. "You thought — ?"

"That you and Dooley messed up on purpose. That you ordered me away from Emil and Ada Firebourne until you could kill them. That you tried to burn Frees to death — you don't even know about that, do you? That you either strong-armed Niles to shoot at me this morning, or that you did it yourself and ran back here to clean the gun. But you didn't know about that, either, did you?"

He licked his lips. "God."

I was on a roll. This man had blasted Jon and me but good when we'd come to town. "Why wouldn't I think those things? You pretended that you knew what you were doing and you knew what was going on. I misjudged you. You were only guarding your turf. You never knew half what was going on, and you never knew what you were doing."

I had him, and he knew it. He looked like Jon had in this very office, not so long ago: like a good lawman ashamed of doing a bad job. Finally he said, "What convinced you I was innocent?"

Nothing, yet. But he hadn't grabbed for any guns since I started talking, and that was a good sign. Besides, things fit better without him. "Motive. Sheriffs don't get rich and don't invest in granaries or anything else."

"You got that right." He settled back. "And next election I hand this desk to someone else. Lately it's been too much work for the money."

I thought of Jon, putting in his years at Homicide and never ceasing to complain, but never quitting. "Plenty of time to say that before the election." I gestured at the handgun in the Baggie. "I took that from a man who may come in to talk to you."

He nodded. "A man named — ?"

"Something I'll leave in my glove compartment. He wants to come in for himself."

Farrell's eyebrows jumped, then plunged. "Think this is a damn game? Did he try to kill you?"

"Twice. He was the bomber. And he had help. He won't tell me who, but he will tell you — if you let him."

He glared at me. "In other words, you're trying to make me do this your way."

"That's right. Arrest him now and he won't say a word. Talk to him, and you'll get it all. He wouldn't tell me; I'm from out of town."

Farrell nodded. "You're learning. Anything else?"

"Sure." This was where he'd shoot me. "I found out where Swenson and Keller and the rest are."

"Where?" He was on his feet. "Dammit, I had Danny Lowenbach on the carpet for two hours yesterday and didn't get anything but I'm-sorries. How'd you — ?" He stopped. "The fella with the gun?"

"That's right. They're at Niles's hunting lodge on the Zumbro River. If I have to guess, I'd say that's the patch of land Sammy Detweiler wanted to buy, back when he planned an irrigation company."

"You work for the *News-Messenger*? That was a couple years back." He paused. "If you clean this one up, I'll be grateful. Sammy soured on Niles big when that deal fell through, and I never figured out why he was so upset. Other people have held out on Sammy and he never got like that."

This was my final test piece. "Niles shot at him." According to Arlis, Farrell hadn't known about that. He wouldn't think Niles could have shot at Sammy. If Arlis was right about this, I could bank on the rest of her information. I waited.

"Oh, you just went too far there, Nathan." He chuckled. "I had Niles's rifle back then. Not legal, but smart. There's a story you don't know —"

"I know it." So Farrell really was innocent, or an incredibly steel-nerved actor, and Arlis Schmidt was probably right about everything else she'd told me. "Niles had a second rifle. That's why he let you take the first one away from him."

I had two reasons to enjoy his expression. Finally he shut up and noticed I was still in front of the desk. I said, "I'd always heard the Marines could beat the Navy."

"Not all of 'em. Being a sergeant helps your vocabulary. So, what are you going to do now?" And he was testing me. I think he realized that I had him.

"Well, there's a man coming here to clear everything up." I glanced around. "And I don't see any deputies —"

"You haven't seen a damn deputy since you got here." He glanced automatically at his belly, caught my eye and glared. "You figure you've got me over a barrel, don't you? I could bust you for withholding evidence and go to that cabin myself."

"Sure you could. But who'd talk to the man coming in?" If he came in. If I got through the next few hours alive and Homer skipped without talking, I'd be in real trouble.

"The town cops."

"You don't trust them to do it. And you can't send them to the country, can you? And it's not a job for the state highway patrol, either." I held my breath. If he was on good terms with the Staters, he might call them anyway. "Not till you know who you're arresting for what," I finished feebly.

It worked. Farrell thumped the desk. "God damnit, I'll go out there and leave a note for your fella to wait for me."

"Like hell you will. Someone's coming in to confess to two attempted murders, plus he'll tie somebody to the biggest string of unsolved murders you've ever had, and you'll go out of town for the morning?" But I hardly needed to say it; he knew. If he missed Homer's confession and the papers got wind of it later — and I'd see to it they did — Gordon County would have a new sheriff.

He said quietly, "Why did you set me up like this?"

I said as quietly, "Because I couldn't trust you." Maybe I could, now, but it was better keeping him tied to his desk.

After a moment he sagged. "You wanna go to the cabin with a badge, or without?"

"Without." I leaned forward. "If I wore a badge, I might have to arrest somebody, no matter what. But there are four innocent people out there, or comparatively innocent, and one crazy. If I can't figure out which one is the crazy, I'm leaving again. Deputy can't do that."

He nodded, relieved. "And I can follow you out there."

"Wish you would."

"Glad to. Wish I could follow you closer, like maybe in

front of you. What if he takes you while you're in the woods? You'd be hard to find.''

I reached into my pocket, and he moved. "No — wait.'' I pulled out a small bottle. "Anise." I opened it, poured a little on my sock. Then I took off the sock and pulled out the handkerchief I'd tucked there. "Didn't you say Daisy was a good sniffer?" I left it on his desk and put my sock back on.

He looked at it distrustfully. "That'll prob'ly kill her. But it should work. You know, don't you, that if your buddy that's coming in to confess takes too long, Daisy'd be a little late finding you.''

"Sure.'' And I was hoping that wouldn't happen. "Give me directions to the place.''

"Surprised you need 'em.'' But he gave them. "You need a gun?''

"No, thanks; I've got —" And I stopped feeling superior. "Look, I'm not shooting anybody today. I'm just carrying it. No shootouts. Okay?''

"I could take your gun away.''

"You could try.'' I looked at him again and conceded, "You could do it. I really wish you wouldn't.''

He considered. "All right. But if you decide to use it, you'd better have a damn good reason. Got that? Good. Get out.''

And he didn't look at me. I walked out, feeling silly. What had I expected — applause, thanks, medals? I'd come in, told him I'd thought he was a killer, withheld evidence, outmaneuvered him, and now I was getting in his way, and there was nothing he could do about it. I was lucky he didn't shoot me in the back.

I turned back around. "Sheriff —"

"Yes?" I think I startled him. Mostly he got called Josh.

"Remember I didn't make this trouble, just found it. I knew where to look.''

" 'Course.'' He was puzzled. Why was I doing this?

"And — look, people around here think you're a hell of

a cop. I can't disagree with them. After this is over, I'll buy you a beer.''

He looked at me for a while, and then he smiled. "Thanks. I hope you can, Nate. I truly hope you can."

Either he wasn't thirsty or he wasn't optimistic. I said, "Remember to check my glove compartment," and left.

Chapter Twenty-Three

I drove past the Zumbro River — not because I'd missed it, though that would have been easy, but to avoid being spotted from the cabin. From the road you could just see the roof; dull gray shingles, probably with a phony wood pattern. If there were any gaps in the bushes near the cabin, someone could be watching from the window.

I parked thirty feet past the point where the woodlot met the road. It was gorgeous in there: ferns, gooseberry bushes, even the weed we used to call Indian pipe, its little segmented hollow stems perfect for a toy pipe stem. The woods were damp. The ferns were brown and dying, but green close to the ground. All around them were maple and walnut and even burr-oak leaves. I'd sound like a parade trying to sneak through that.

Cities are easy. You wear soft soles if you want, but mostly you stand around with a bunch of other people, not looking much different, watching your target and moving up slowly. I've gotten so I can walk right next to someone before they realize I'm following them, if the street's busy. All it takes is a good sense of window-shopping, or an intent look directed at someone else. I was back where there were no windows and no shops, and up ahead someone wanted to kill me.

On my pad I wrote, "Homer Cortland," and Annie's name and phone number with a message. I hated putting her name in writing, but Farrell already knew it; she'd dealt herself in. I had to end things today.

I walked the ditch to the far side of the lot, then slipped between strands of barbed wire and walked up the fields. It hadn't been planted this year — probably part of Niles's farm subsidy. I slogged through drying Timothy grass, edging as close to the cockleburrs and elderberries at the edge of the field as I could. I didn't want to be spotted from the road, either. A good man with a deer rifle could pick me off the road or the neighboring farm — either one. I was glad I had a brown coat, and I took off my too-dark hat.

When I finally cut through the woods I noticed that I was sweating. At least there weren't any bees to attract. I stepped carefully over sticks and around loose piles of leaves, trying to step in the dampest places. I was doing the reverse of what any sane person does in woods, but it was working; my shoes were sopping and muck-ridden, but my footsteps were quiet. Soggy leaves don't rustle.

I startled a pheasant, but not as much as it startled me. I hoped nobody in the lodge was listening; probably you could hear it flapping off squawking for miles. I went back to crouching, peering ahead more carefully. I didn't see any other animals, but I hadn't seen the pheasant, either.

I came out of the brush near the Zumbro. The bank here was seven or eight feet high, and the bend was wide. Probably the water was a good diving depth. Someone had stuck a telephone pole into the earth at an angle so that the top hung over the water. A hay rope was suspended from it. Swinging out on that must have been fun in the summer. I wished it was June, and I was twelve.

And that was the last thing I thought, as something hit behind my ear, and the landscape swayed sideways.

Chapter Twenty-Four

I heard arguing nearby in a foreign language. I wanted to sleep. I was a kid again, with a fever. Then I was a grown-up with a colossal hangover, probably from one of Bernie's parties, and people were talking downstairs. I caught every third or fourth word, even if they didn't make sense: "call," "fault," "over," "him."

Then I remembered the river and falling sideways. My head hurt like hell. I'm not a fighter, and I don't get knocked out often; the feeling wasn't familiar. I hoped it wouldn't ever be.

One of the voices said, "Think that'll hold him?"

"It'll hold anything," Niles Swenson said. "I tie deer to fenders."

"I wanna know what we do from here," someone — Cavanaugh? — said.

"You always wanna know something." That was Frees. "We'll find out soon. Be nice if we could just leave him here when we go, not hurt him." He sounded regretful already. So much for Frees's moral resolve.

"We gotta talk to him."

"Sammy, you're crazy."

"Hey, no names. We gotta talk to him, is all." I heard movement toward me. "Maybe he can get us out of this."

"Sam, you're a dreamer." It was Niles again. "I take him, I kill him, we go on out of here, maybe nobody knows we were here, right?" His accent, under stress, was thicker.

I opened my eyes, then nearly pulled them shut. I didn't know light hurt like that.

"You okay, Nate?" Frees squatted down by my face. "You took a hefty blow." He looked sideways at Swenson, who snorted.

"I've been better." The words slurred. I tried to stretch out, realized that it wasn't armrests or the end of the bed cramping me; Swenson had put a noose around my neck and run a line down to my feet, just short enough so that I wouldn't be able to stand. I lifted my right hand, and my left came with it. Great. If I was going to get out of here, I'd have to talk my way out.

"Lemme sit you up." Frees twisted me around. My head twinged. "Feel pretty rocky, huh?" he said sympathetically.

"Right." I added, "I hear you're talking about killing me?" I tried to make it casual, and watch reactions, Niles's most of all.

He folded his arms. "Sure, that's right." And I suddenly felt better.

"You're bluffing."

"I don't —"

I shook my head. Bad move. I tried to hold it with my bound hands; the best I could do was prop it against the heels of my palms. "Hang on a sec. Okay. Niles, you put the gas can in Frees's bonfire. None of these others would be that good at stalking. And you put it in too far back, and before Frees finished the pile; you were hoping he'd notice it."

He didn't say anything. "And you turned down the job

of shooting me this morning. You'd be the first person . . .
anyone . . . would ask.''

"That's for sure," Sammy muttered.

"You didn't do in Ada Firebourne, because you'd never
have left the reins dangling, and you'd have been more
alert about the spilled straw. Trackers check tracks." He
nodded, impressed. "So quit saying you're gonna kill me.
Somebody else here will, but not you."

I looked around. They looked desperate, upset. I don't
suppose I looked much better.

"We've gotta kill you," Frees said pleadingly. "You
found us —"

"I know. And I think you could kill me if someone
pushed you into it. You can be pushed, can't you? But I
don't think you'd start it." He dropped his eyes. I
wondered if he were ashamed of being only an accessory,
of being too weak for anything else.

I looked at the others: Virgil Keller, Sammy Detweiler,
Kevin Riley. A man I didn't recognize might be Ed Parker.
Pat Cavanaugh was in the corner, sitting in a wood-frame,
vinyl-cushioned chair that matched the sofa I was on. Over
the wood stove next to him was a horizontal board with
five antlers and space for a sixth on it. Nice place.

Riley said, unexpectedly, "We have to talk." He didn't
sound as much like a high-pressure salesman as he wanted
to. "We got in way over our heads."

"All of you?" I almost shook my head again. "I can't
buy that. One of you started it, probably by cutting a deal
you didn't have the grain for. The others followed. Which
one — ?"

Most of them looked at the floor. Sammy looked, even
more viciously, at Niles. "Figures. You wouldn't worry
about what happened to the granary, Niles, if you could
protect your damn land. You wanted out anyway."

He looked down at me with contempt. "You're not so
smart. I was the first in this bunch, yah. But I didn't do
half what was done."

My head hurt, and I didn't have much time to figure out what was going on. "I know. The car bomber had help from Virgil or Kevin — Kevin, I think."

"Just the parts," he said anxiously. "And, well, I got the charge from Dooley. But I didn't put it in your car, and I didn't know what it was for till I got the timer from —" He stopped.

"I know. I talked to Homer. By the way, Niles, he's a lousy shot. You should have done it yourself."

"I bet you I would've got you first shot."

"Nope. You wouldn't do it. And you didn't set the granary fire, either." I turned to Ed Parker. "That was you. He would've asked Virgil, but Virgil would've just done another bomb, and they're easy to detect. Nothing like having a chemist on a string, is there?"

Ed nodded. "You can't prove it."

"You bet I can't. Any money you used a chemical that would show up as a by-product of a fungicide, or a pesticide, or something some farmer accidentally soaked the grain in, or a by-product of fermenting grain. And you doused the tops of each bin with it, without settling the suspended particles or having to depend on them."

"Two or three would be enough. The others would catch." He was being cautious, but he suddenly added, "But I didn't — I wouldn't ever have done that to Emil. That's — that's —"

"Sick. Right. But it always looked like you were buying silence, each time somebody died or nearly died, right? Emil would have talked. His other investments really were secure, and he figured he could take a loss and get out. The first time, he tried to hire an investigator to come down and find out who was embezzling. So you — maybe just Frees, maybe all of you — hired Colfax to kill Roy. That scared Emil good; he stayed quiet two whole years. Probably he was forced to plow his money back into the granary, just to make sure he couldn't pull out again. When Colfax died, Firebourne panicked — and somebody killed Ada, to warn him. Just a little closer to killing him, enough to silence him but not look connected with the granary. That was dumb. Emil loved her.'' They all looked sick, and I was troubled. My head hurt, and I was close to the answer if I could just clear my mind. God, I was sleepy.

Riley said, unexpectedly, "You've gotta help us." Niles opened his mouth. Riley whirled. "Dammit, we can't go on. It's all out in the open. We gotta figure out what to do now."

"What to do?" What could I say? However reasonable I was, one person in here was too psychotic to buy it.

"You don't understand." That was Sammy, hands spread in front of him. "Look at us. We built this town. Hell, by now we *are* this town. Between us we own two-thirds of Main Street. We don't wanna ruin everything."

"And you don't want to be ruined?" I tried to think. "I don't think there's any way out. Maybe you could kill me, but I told the sheriff I was coming out here. He's following." It was out. Now I might be killed. "You'd better figure out what to do, fast. Do you want to go on, killing people, burning things, fighting your way out?"

They none of them looked at each other. I didn't need an answer, and suddenly I was very afraid. None of these men were crazy enough to go on. I very badly wanted to believe that you had to be crazy to get this far.

Unexpectedly, Frees said, "Look, if it was just us —"

"But it's not, huh?" And I understood. "It never was. My God, Danny Lowenbach could talk you into anything. Did he do any of the work himself?" And I realized that I already knew. "Emil and Ada. None of you could have killed them. He was trying to scare you all. Did a good job, didn't he?"

Virgil said, too loudly, "Well, that's sure the damn end of this. You bastards can stay and hang; I'm going." He strode to the door.

Niles moved to stop him, then shrugged and let him go. "Now we sure better talk."

I looked from one of them to the other. "Not much to talk about. Run, like Virgil, or give yourselves up. That's all the choices." I tried to sound casual. "Personally, I'd recommend giving up."

They were wavering, but they were starting to look relieved. These had never been hardened men. It was amazing that anyone — even Danny Lowenbach — could have talked them into the things they'd done. Probably he'd pushed on one of them at a time, always picking the man who was most financially strapped at the moment.

Unexpectedly, it was Niles who gave in first. "Sure. Okay, we'll quit here." He grinned weakly, the last of his bluster. "Wish you'd been the kind of talker Lowenbach was. Could have done this earlier."

He moved toward the table to pick up the hunting knife. I hoped he was going to cut the ropes.

We heard a scuffling outside. "Someone's there," Sammy said with fear in his voice.

The door opened, and Danny Lowenbach walked in, in a padded shooting jacket and carrying a pump shotgun. "Boy, I thought I'd never find you guys." He smiled reassuringly.

The others looked relieved, and I knew that I'd lost them.

"Danny!" Frees was babbling. He'd always been the easiest for Danny to work with. "Virgil ran away."

"Oh, no." Danny grinned. "I talked some sense into him. He's waiting for the rest of you. We'll get out of this okay, if we keep our heads."

The others stood listening. Danny was still smiling, still relaxed and normal, but I couldn't buy it. Talk sense to Virgil? Virgil wouldn't listen, not to sense or to anything else. There'd been too many times he'd have been useful if he hadn't been so stubborn that Danny had gone to someone else: the gas can fire, the bomb, even Roy's murder.

And I looked at Danny, smiling and acting like everything was normal, and suddenly I was very afraid. His investors would listen to him. He knew how to talk to them, tell them what they needed to hear; he always had. And Danny had just killed Virgil.

"You all look so worried," he laughed. "Scared of going to jail?" He moved from one side of the door to the other, but stayed between them and the door. "Nobody's going to jail."

Swenson muttered, "This I gotta hear," but everyone else waited expectantly. Danny looked over at Swenson, and I shifted quietly to the edge of the sofa. I knew I'd never find my gun, and I was tied far too well to fight.

Danny stepped back in the door, and for a moment the sun, through a side window, caught his face: still boyish, bright-eyed, optimistic. The kind of man you want to see make it. But there were dark bags under his eyes. He'd put in lots of extra time lately.

Ed Parker said suddenly, "The gun butt." Everyone looked.

Danny, untroubled, said, "What?" He raised it up, looking at it curiously. "It's just a gun butt. Like the jacket?"

But Kevin saw it, too. "There's hair on it." And there was: a single swatch of it, caught in the swivel for the sling. Virgil's hair. Danny must have missed it when he cleaned the butt.

"There is?" Danny looked at it curiously, barrel drifting forward as he turned the gun. "How 'bout that." And the change, the sudden enthusiasm in his voice, was all the hint I needed.

I dropped off the couch as he swung the barrel up. I struck my head, hard, on the original sore place. Purple spots swam in front of my eyes, but I couldn't pass out yet.

Once, long ago, I'd dropped to the floor in another room and rolled toward a man with a gun. This time I was completely helpless. I rolled under the sofa as far as I could and hoped that adrenaline alone could keep my eyes open.

With the first blast of the gun I heard Danny's voice,

shouting over the cries of the people who had trusted him: "I been blind." Bang. "I been foolish." Bang. "I coulda had it all, and I hadda stay here." Bang.

He yelled for five shots. He must have had one shell in the breech. He'd emptied the gun, but nobody was going to run up and stop him now.

Finally there was silence. I lay under the couch, holding my breath. I remembered stories from Chicago, years ago, when Richard Speck killed eight nurses while a ninth rolled under the bed and hid. Speck lost count.

I saw the shotgun barrel swing down. I half-shut my eyes. It poked Ed Parker in the back of the neck, then receded. I heard Danny walking around, poking the others, calling their names. Even now, at the end, he was too nervous to sit down. The feet stopped, stock-still, near the center of the room. Ah, God, I thought wretchedly, he's counting. He's thinking of the names he's called. He knows I'm here. Here it comes, right through the cushions. I heard him reload, and I waited to see the cushions flame apart, the last thing I'd see.

Instead of shooting and silence, there was only silence. Then Danny said softly, relief in his voice, "Yes. Yes, I would like that." There was another shotgun blast, this one louder, and the gun sped by my eyes, skittering butt-first across the floor.

Then there were two thuds as Danny Lowenbach's knees hit the floor, and he sagged like a marionette being thrown in the box. Most of the rest of him followed. He must have put the gun barrel in his mouth.

I lay still, gradually breathing louder, but no slower. No one else made any noise. How could they?

I still didn't crawl out from under the sofa. There was no point. People were getting killed out there; it wasn't safe. It would never be safe. I'd wait here until Farrell arrived —

It came to me, vaguely, that Farrell might be a while. Even after he finished with Homer, he and Daisy would find Virgil on the way to the cabin. There was no way that dog would miss a fresh corpse. Farrell might decide to go back to his police car and call an ambulance before checking further. I still didn't crawl out; I didn't want to look, no matter how long I had to wait.

Then I heard a groan. Weak as it was, it hung in the air forever, full of pain and sorrow, impossible to ignore.

The rope between my neck and my legs slowed me down; I could only edge forward an inch or two at a time. I could roll over, but if I landed wrong I might strangle. I concentrated on getting every inch of play that rope had.

The groaning man was Sammy. For all his anger at Niles, he'd been partly shielded by the big man's body. Only partly; his midsection was a mess. He groaned, and his hands moved across his shirt.

By the time I got next to him I was soaked in blood; the trip across the cabin floor had gotten worse with each minute. He turned his head with difficulty. "You're dead."

"Are you all right?" That didn't even sound stupid to me. My head felt like a balloon where I'd restruck it. I was sleepless and fuzzy and probably in shock. "Rest easy. Can you untie me?" I thought of walking back to the car, driving for help. I couldn't have made it to the road, and if I had I couldn't have driven as far as the left-hand ditch.

His hands fluttered on the ropes, then collapsed. "Ropes." He spoke clearly, but his words sounded as though they were coming from some new part of his brain that wasn't quite sure what to do with them.

I knelt, Japanese fashion, which took tension off my ropes. "You want your head up?" Moving him didn't much matter any more.

He didn't answer, and I stared down at him. His eyes were focusing and unfocusing, now pin-prick pupils, now a belladonna patient. As I lifted his head in my bound hands, I stared down at him. I couldn't believe he was still alive.

Then I heard a groan from another end of the room. I looked around wildly. "Pat? Pat?"

There wasn't a repeat. But Cavanaugh had been well back from the door; there might be a chance.

Sammy gasped, and I looked back down. His head rolled from side to side and his lips moved, but little came out. He was barely conscious. That meant I should do something, but I couldn't remember what.

I wanted him to talk, to tell me everything was all right. I guess I told him so. He did talk, as best he could. I don't think he even knew I was there. I wasn't too sure, either, and the more he talked the worse it got.

He shifted, and something fell out onto my hand, right from his shirt. A pellet. I stared at it stupidly. "How many of these are in you?"

"A hundred thousand. Stars. They rise by night. You check the bank some time, see if I'm not right. They rise by night, while you're not looking; you can't pay 'em. They're about half full of dirt. We're all half dirt. Danny says we'll have to burn 'em. They're burning now. I can feel them."

I tried shifting him around, but I was clumsy. His head slid to the floor, and he cried out.

"That's the bottom. They say it hurts at the bottom, but it's hell in the middle. The middle is where he got me, but I couldn't stay there. Can you feel me sliding? Please tell me I'm not sliding. I wake up in the night and I know I'm gone. Please tell me. Please don't tell my mother."

I said he wasn't and I wouldn't and he was going to be all right.

"That's right," he said, he voice suddenly strong. "Little things like this, a man gets through it all. Hell, nobody cries over a few losses. "Nobody cried over Colfax, did they? Goddamn sniveler . . . Danny, Danny, you shot the bees into me. I didn't mean it, I didn't do it, I know I watched, but I couldn't call it quits. Give me something. Not that, something."

I told him he was all right again. I told him there weren't any bees. I told him I didn't know what to do.

"Get away. This town's gone sick. Broken hearts are following me down the street. Another drink? What the hell. For Chrissake, think of the kids. Next time payments fall due, I swear I'll tell everything. I won't tell a thing. Anything. It's a sure thing. I could let you in on it." He sounded hopeful, and he reached up with one crooked hand and grabbed my shirt. "Right on the ground floor, and all it takes is some cash up front. The cash. You'll be rich. Give us the cash, tomorrow. Sure. Sure. Trust me. Hey, call Gary; he wouldn't want to miss this, would he?" He let go of me and said, suddenly happy, "I wouldn't miss this for the world. Give me cash any day." He added, in a different voice, "Give me some water, the only thing that I want."

His head sank, and I picked him up. "Is that what you want? Water? Tell me. You want water?"

"Don't shake me."

"You want water?" I was shaking him again; I saw myself this time, my tied hands pulling his coat together. I let him down slowly. "I'll get it if you want. You want it?"

"Nothing left. A few good friends at the end. What a deal. Friends together, millionaires. You could spend a hundred bucks a drink and never go dry." His eyes cleared for a moment, but I don't think he saw me. "Dry. Jesus, so dry and gone. Water. Just a little. Thousand bucks a drink. The only thing I want."

I set his head down and started crawling. I was at the sink in two minutes. These clothes were never going to be good for anything again. Even if they came clean I'd get rid of them. I pulled myself up the cabinets and held on; I could stand on tiptoe, but not balance myself. I filled a glass, slopped about a third of it over getting it to the floor, spilled a little more on the way to Sammy.

I called to him and shouted at him, and finally I shook him, but he was dead. All that work for a man that died thirsty. I put his head in my lap. I guess that's when I started to cry.

Some time after that a man with a dog on a leash came through the front door. I didn't catch what he said, or what I answered.

Chapter Twenty-Five

The tough, cynical detective woke up hours later in a hospital room, hardly a scratch on him.

My first official returning act was to look for my gun. They were smart not to leave it with me. After that I read my phone messages and my one card (hand-drawn by Annie, of Marlowe upending my fridge into his mouth), and rang for the nurse.

I pointed to the card. "The woman that left this — has she been by?"

"Not yet today. She'll be in just before the end of visiting hours. Takes time to get here from Minneapolis."

"Here? I'm in Belle View?"

"I'll get your doctor." She did, too. Dr. Sloane, or at least that's what his name tag said, sat on the edge of the bed and talked as though we were old friends. Maybe we were.

"So, Nate, you remember everything." He thumbed one of my eyes while I thought of my answer.

"I remember enough. I'm short some time, I think. Is this the day after —?"

"It's after you went out to Swenson's cabin, yes." Nice oblique way to put it. "And you remember events there?"

Some. "All but how I got here. Did the sheriff — ?"

"Farrell, and Daisy, and an ambulance. He went back to the main road and called two wagons, one for a body and one for the survivors. There's a man that could call horse races, if he were a betting man."

"What did I do?"

He looked at me frankly. "You cried. They found you crying, cradling a dead man on your lap, and the sheriff did the same for you until the ambulance crew came. They radioed me, and we did some quick guessing and sedated you." While talking he thumbed my other eye, checked my tongue, had the nurse take my pulse and pressure, and made me feel agreeably frail. "When they first saw you, they thought you were bleeding —" He caught himself. "Feeling okay?"

Dead. "Weak."

"Not surprising. We got your medical records that night; I'd figured you wouldn't react to the sedative, and your concussion, if you had one, wasn't serious. I'm a betting man, too."

"Next time can some other horse run, and I'll sit and bet? What concussion?"

"Concussion, shock and exhaustion. Some blood loss; your hand opened up. Somebody hit you on the head — whoa. Easy. What do you remember?"

Pat. "There's somebody alive in that cabin —"

"Relax. He's at the Mayo Clinic." Sloane sighed. "Kidney, spleen, some other parts full of shot. Heavy blood loss, or we might have tried to do it here. Still, we're not that far from the Mayo by ambulance. He'll live to stand trial."

I didn't say anything. I hoped I could miss the trial.

"Nate, did you go out on me again?"

"Huh? No, no; just thinking. How's the town taking the news?"

"Rough. Those clowns represented the stablest money in town; hell, Firebourne alone brought in more investors to that operation than I care to think. The granary's dead, of course. A couple of banks may go with it. Most of the farmers only needed something like this to go belly-up."

"I guess I'm not too popular."

"Nobody's too upset with *you*. To them you're just a natural force, like a tornado or a drought. But those damned bastards who set us —" He caught himself. "Sorry. That was where I had half my savings."

I winced. Chances were I'd hear that a lot on the way out of town. "Everybody feels like you do about them?"

"Even the ones that didn't invest. Cavanaugh has a police guard on him at Mayo's; one of the Detweiler kids — he's a farmer southeast of town, lost it all and had a stroke this last week — says he'll finish Cavanaugh before the trial."

"Revenge."

"Or justice."

"Can you tell the difference? Outside a court, I mean?"

"Well, courts aren't always just . . . mmm. You ask tough questions, for a man that's been asleep for two days."

"Two days? I've been lying here —? Gimme a phone."

I got one. "Annie? Oh, God, Annie, I'm sorry. I tried at home, I just wanted you to know I'm all —"

"Nate." She made a ragged sound I hadn't expected. "You're all right. I came to see you yesterday —"

"You did?" Uh-oh. "I don't remember."

"I know. We talked, but mostly I listened. You told me about Marlowe, and your father's heart attack, and being thirsty —"

"Look, it's over. I'm sorry if I upset you."

"Are you okay? Really okay?"

"Let's say I'm not as good as I get, but if you tell me

something today, chances are I'll know it tomorrow."

So she told me something short. And sweet. I remembered it. I'll probably remember it again tomorrow.

I said I loved her, too, and that I hadn't meant to scare her. "I expected a mess down here, and you knew I was tense, but I didn't think it would be like this." I glanced around the room. Sloane was studiously catching up on last month's *Time*. The nurse was openly gloating, and a candy-striper was in tears. "Look, maybe we should finish this in private. Dr. Sloane, can I check out today?"

"If I don't find anything, in about an hour."

"Terrific. Annie, I'll be up in the Cities in three hours. Where can I meet you?"

"The library. I've been at my desk till I heard from you. Nate, you sound so good —"

"Don't cry. You're tougher than I am."

"That's why I was so worried." But she sounded better. "Your damn cat's fine, too. He scratched me."

"Bastard." Sloane dropped his magazine, and the candy-striper gasped. "I'll see you, Annie."

So I hung up and lay quietly for a while until Sloane said acidly that he could remove grins, too, mostly by billing. They gave me my clothes — they'd had the foresight to get them from the hotel, and to keep them where I couldn't find them — and I submitted to more prodding and mind testing. When they asked, I told them who the president was and, for kicks, who it should be, and they agreed wholeheartedly and threw me out.

I walked to the sheriff's office, a good ten blocks. I was wobbly but passable, if I didn't have to run. The air was chilly and crisp; I felt as though I could almost see my breath. I was glad I could look for it.

The car was fine. I inspected under the hood and beneath the car, then beneath the dash. I signed a receipt for it, which the dispatcher kept — I wondered why until I checked the mileage on it; someone went joy riding. I rolled down the road.

When I was nearly out of town I turned back, crossed over two blocks and stopped at the abandoned railroad tracks. The garden was bare now, all the bushes shrouded and most of the other plants pulled or cut off. The lawn was immaculate.

"Mrs. Schmidt?" She looked up from the windmill. "Are you painting that, or what?"

"Just primer on the vanes. A new coat helps it through the winter." She straightened. "I hear you have all your business done, Mr. Phillips."

"I certainly do, and thank you for your help. Without you I might be dead somewhere." I coughed. "I hope no one you know was badly hurt by this."

"Hope." She shook her head. "Hope is a wonderful thing, young man. We have it even when we know better." She turned and smiled at me, and I could see how red-rimmed her eyes were. "Children of my friends, children that used to play in this garden. That's who died. That's who's poor. They played in this garden."

She bent down suddenly and wrenched up some dried stems. I said lamely, "It is a pretty garden. I bet they loved it."

"Of course they did." She blinked very rapidly, and her wrinkled cheeks quivered along with her thin lips. "Do you know, the other day the mayor came by and asked if it was all right if we moved this garden to the city park on my death? That the city promised to keep it up almost as well as I had?" She accented the "almost." "Frank has always been such a polite boy. I said yes."

She wiped her eyes without pulling her glasses off. I don't think she saw smudges well any more. "You make your garden as pretty as you can, and you fence it to keep things out, but you can't keep children out. And afterward you watch them, and they get hurt."

"I'm sorry. They weren't children any more."

"How can you tell?" It was the angriest she'd sounded. "When did you stop being a child? When did you last cry like one, fight like one, want like one?"

There wasn't much I could say to that. She went on. "The Lord says one must be like a little child to enter the kingdom of heaven. Some folks think he was saying, 'Be innocent.' I think he was saying, 'Don't pretend you're a grown up.' "

I thought of Bernie and how happy he was, how happy he made people. I thought about Dave and his sad, big eyes and good heart. I reached for the homemade card in my breast pocket, thinking about Annie, and about crying.

"Mrs. Schmidt, if it's any comfort, I think I've learned a lot here. Not enough, but a lot." I coughed. "What happened here was only just. You were right about justice. It's a terrible thing. I'm sorry."

She smiled at me with friendly concern and walked jerkily over to pat my arm. "No harm done — no, that's not true. Let's say you meant no harm, and nobody hates you." She wagged a finger at me. "I hear you have a lovely young woman."

"I guess so."

"You guess." Her teasing voice was back. "You ought to be doing more than guess, young man. What are you doing, wasting a beautiful afternoon talking to an old woman like me?"

"Talking to you is never a waste. You're a lovely woman yourself."

"Oh, now." She turned her head in mock exasperation. "You men say such things."

I opened the gate for her and escorted her to the house. She stopped and glared at the silver maple again. The wind had taken its toll; the tree was all but barren.

"What is it this time?" I honestly didn't know.

"The last leaf." She shook her head. "I know it's coming."

I looked at her poised rake. "And you're ready for it. May I come see your garden in the spring?"

"Oh, please do. I'd like that. Though I can't guarantee I'll still be here, you know."

"I can't imagine what could take you away from us."

"Such talk!" She laughed, the specter of a girl's giggle. "God takes us all, Nathan. We are each as a blade of grass, that is cut down and thrown into an oven and baked." She stared back at the tree and added, with frank envy. "And He never misses a one. I don't see how He does it."

I closed the door behind her and walked to the car, trying not to seem in a hurry. If I hit the road early enough, I'd get to the library early. I was betting Annie would, too.

FREE!!
BOOKS BY MAIL
CATALOGUE

BOOKS BY MAIL will share with you our current bestselling books as well as hard to find specialty titles in areas that will match your interests. You will be updated on what's new in books at no cost to you. Just fill in the coupon below and discover the convenience of having books delivered to your home. *PLEASE ADD $1.00 TO COVER THE COST OF POSTAGE & HANDLING.*

BOOKS BY MAIL

In the U.S. –
210 5th Ave., 7th Floor
New York, N.Y., 10010

320 Steelcase Road E.,
Markham, Ontario L3R 2M1

Please send Books By Mail catalogue to:

Name_____
    (please print)

Address_____

City_____

Prov._____Postal Code_____

(BBM1)